The Other Side of Life

Alfred Jendrasik

AuthorHouse™
1663 Liberty Drive, Suite 200
Bloomington, IN 47403
www.authorhouse.com
Phone: 1-800-839-8640

© 2007 Alfred Jendrasik. All rights reserved.

No part of this book may be reproduced, stored in a retrieval system, or transmitted by any means without the written permission of the author.

First published by AuthorHouse 11/6/2007

ISBN: 978-1-4343-3148-9 (sc)

Printed in the United States of America
Bloomington, Indiana

This book is printed on acid-free paper.

My mom and dad, Alfred and Bertha Jendrasik
My brother Michael Jendrasik and family
My brother Robert Jendrasik and family
My sister Mary Wittig and family
My sons Aaron and Joshua Jendrasik and families
My granddaughter Allura Jendrasik
My grandson Aaron Jendrasik A.J.
My friends Barry Dry and family
Mark Mingrino and family
John Skocz and David Leathers
And a special thanks to Bravo restaurants for their help and support.

In Memory of Alfred Jendrasik

      you know
this man by man names, Al, Fred, Fef, Dad and pap
      he is far, far away on a distant star
          but do no stare
              nor fear
          but show others you care
         you know
              let go
                        let go

You can hear him in the whispering wind
      or on a crashing wave at the beach
          or along a nature trail
              for he was a peaceful man

      and he was a fixer of things
        building
            repairing
                creating

    so no more
        fighting
            hating
                hurting

for he was a peaceful man
  I know you can
      you know
          you know
              you know

The Beach House
Chapter One

THERE WAS SOMETHING OUT THERE, a deep unbelievable feeling lurking somewhere, but I was determined to find it. I began having these strange feelings even as a child. I always knew I was meant to be a writer, but that was all I knew. My greatest struggle was a strong desire to find meaning in my life.

Something had happened to me one day. I was with a large group of people. I was not sure who they were, but it felt as if my spirit had left me and I was in another place. It was dark outside and there were thousands of stars in the sky that spelled out words and phrases, "Straighten out your mind. Have faith in the Lord. He is coming soon." Awaking from a dream, trembling and sweating, these words echoed through my mind. I ignored them, was afraid of them, and did not want to be a part of them, but I could not relax as they gnawed at me like a growling stomach needing to be fed. This was the only dream with words that I ever remembered.

My life was very repetitious. It was the same thing day after day—an organized, dead-end job in which I did articles for a magazine. I got up early in the morning, showered, ate a quick breakfast, ran to catch a bus, and ran across a bridge wishing I could jump off and end this boring life. I was not the only one. Grasping my stomach and feeling very weary, I sat on a bench and took several deep breaths. I felt very nauseated and light-headed. "Oh, God, am I going to be able to handle this task you have planned for me?" Suddenly it drifted away and I was fine.

I spent most of my free time reading the newspaper. There were so many lonely and unhappy people in the world unsatisfied with their lives. There were single males and females, married couples, divorced couples, seniors, and people from all denominations. Some of them were religious, some with no beliefs, and others who did not care and had completely given up. I always had a heart for these types of people and wished I could help them. I even started playing the lotto and thought that maybe if I had enough money, I could help them, but there were many rich people just as unhappy as everyone else. It was getting late and I had plans of meeting my best friend, Colin, at the boat docks. Taking a bus to town, I crossed a small bridge to the boardwalk. I sat on a wooden bench and looked at a picture of a beach house.

Suddenly Colin circled around the crowds toward me. The wind tossed his long, dark hair and made his shirt look like a huge balloon and his baggy shorts resemble clown pants. Clutching a black bag, he sat next to me.

"Did you get some new photos?" I observed, watching him flip through them.

"Yes, I got some good bargains. Look at these pictures of Liz Taylor, Elvis, Marilyn Monroe, and James Dean!" he exclaimed.

"Very nice," I answered, unthrilled

"Joah, what is wrong?"

"I just have a lot on my mind," I answered, grasping the picture of the beach house.

Colin looked over my shoulder at the picture in my hand. "Where did you get that picture of that decrepit house?"

"I inquired about it, not sure if I can ever own it, but I would like to try to purchase it."

"Why? Where is it at?"

"On Padre Island, beachside."

"Why would you want to live in the middle of nowhere?"

Standing up and looking below, I stared at all of the people on the lower deck. I watched as they loaded canoes, skiing apparel, water crafts, bikes, and cycles from the boardwalk to the back of the ferryboat. "I want to help them."

"Help who?" Colin asked, looking below.

"Just people who are really unhappy and want to leave this earth."

"And what can you do for them?" Colin inquired, grabbing my arm and dragging me through the crowds to the boarding area. As soon as the clerk collected the fee, Colin raced to his favorite spot, comfortable cushioned seats, and saved them for us.

Lagging behind him, I caught up and sat next to him. "I am not sure."

Colin nodded in confusion and changed the subject. "Want to go shopping?"

"No, I am going to see this house."

"What did your parents say about this? What about your job?"

"They feel the same as you do, did not choose this place; it chose me. I quit my job."

A sudden whistle blew and the ferryboat left the dock.

"I thought writing was your entire life."

"That is a part of it, but there is more."

"How will you support yourself?"

I stood up and let the breeze brush through my light-brown hair, let the mist cling to my hairy arms, and breathed in the fresh sea air. "I don't know. I just know that I need a change. There has to be something more for me out there."

"This is not like you to do something so unordinary."

Stroking my facial hair, I faced Colin. "This is ordinary for me. Something happened to me. I was feeling very sad and depressed. I was led to a graveyard. This horrible question came to my mind, "How would you like to be dead?""

"What did you do?" Colin asked, with concern.

"I thought about it, shocked, and I did not want to die! Then, I thought, wait, we have to remember the good these people did, not the evil deeds, and to bury the hurt and anger deep beneath, and never, never dig it up again. I thought about my dead life and decided to make the change."

A sudden wave crashed against the side of the boat and a mist filled the air.

"Is this change making you popular or well known?"
"No, but it makes me feel good about myself."
"Is it making you money?"
"No."
"So why continue with it?
"Why continue with your pictures, collectibles, and junk?"

Colin clung to his pictures and didn't answer.

"All I know is it is like faith, something I can't see, yet believe."

The ferryboat docked on Padre Island, the clerks ushered the guests onto the ramp, and everyone scattered in different directions. Colin took a beach taxi to the mainland shopping area to look for more collectibles. I took a path to the other side of the island and followed the signs. It was a pleasant walk across decks and bridges, tropical jungles, swamps, and rows of palm trees. Following a windy path across dunes, beach grass, and exotic plants, I found the decrepit house nestled in tropical brush and palm trees. The entire house creaked and whistled as the wind brushed across shattered windows, splintered railings, and missing boards around the walkway. Mud and sludge, broken branches, and large leaves lay beneath the slanted stilts. Looking at the house was depressing. I clutched a beach blanket I had tucked away beneath the house and strolled along the shore. I closed my eyes and recalled my first night on the beach. A few weeks ago I brought camping gear, a tent, and a sleeping bag and set everything up on the beach near the dunes. It was wonderful listening to the waves crashing on the shore and awakening to the gulls and seabirds calling and squealing as the sun played over my face. It was the first time I had relaxed in a long time. I felt the same way now. Getting comfortable on the beach blanket, the sun lulled me to sleep. A sudden noise awakened me. Brushing sand from my face and eyes, I noticed someone hovering above me.

"I knew I would find you here," Colin smiled, placing a bag of food on the blanket. Digging the handle of an umbrella into the sand, he dropped his black bag next to it.

"How did you find me?" I wondered, grabbing a can of soda.

"I inquired about the house at the real estate office. They were nice enough to direct me to it. You were not at the house and I figured you must have gone for a walk. I was right," he said, ducking beneath the umbrella.

"Did you find any new collectibles?"

"No," he answered, disappointed, "they sold the one of James Dean that I really wanted. Oh well."

"Why are you here? You hate the beach," I inquired, sitting up and brushing the sand from my clothes.

"You never take time to eat. You worry me."

"That was very thoughtful of you. I am starved."

"I saw the house," Colin said, munching on a sandwich. "It looks like it should be condemned."

"You can't judge a book by its cover," I said, chomping on fries.

"How did you find the old rubble you call a house?"

"There was a bad storm about a week ago. The winds and rain came so hard and caught me off guard. I hid behind a large dune for protection, looked across the beach, and there was the house."

Colin nodded and munched on his sandwich.

"The oddest feeling came over me as I walked to it, déjà vu, as if I had seen this place before in a dream."

"Have you ever walked through it?"

"No, it is locked," I answered, sipping the soda and finishing my lunch.

"Lets do it," Colin insisted, jumping up and throwing his things together.

"No, it is dangerous," I told him, "the floor is shaky and full of holes."

Colin did not listen and raced down the shore.

I quickly snatched up my beach blanket and soda and lagged behind him. When we reached the house, I explained. "There is a ladder we can use. The steps are shaky with missing boards and a loose railing." I directed Colin and held the ladder for him, proceeded behind him, and carefully stepped along the rotted boards and looked inside. There were leaks in the roof, cracked plaster along the walls, and debris on the floor. Some of the skylights were cracked with holes and chipped glass. There were also many French doors and windows with shattered panes and window seals. The most fascinating part was the spiral staircase that led to the bedrooms. The kitchen was unique with a curved corner window circling the new cabinets and counter tops.

"Why would someone leave this place? It looks like they did a lot of remodeling."

"There was a hurricane, which flooded the area and the owners never came back."

"It needs a lot of work," Colin observed, finishing his soda.

"I know a little about doing repairs, but not much."

"Don't look at me. I know nothing, but I could help you decorate it," Colin said, grasping the handle of the sliding door. It was locked. "Do you have keys?"

"No, not yet, but I may have them next week."

Colin kept trying all of the doors and windows, but they were locked or bolted with boards and shutters. He grasped the handle of a large window and it released and opened.

"I am not sure we should go inside. It could be dangerous," I warned, clutching his shoulder, stopping him.

"Maybe you are right," Colin disagreed, removing my hand and jumping through the window.

"Colin, I can't believe you! What is the matter with you? We could fall through the floor," I reprimanded, climbing through the window, carefully stepping to the floor.

"Have we fallen yet?" Colin laughed, dancing.

"No," I said, staring at the warped boards, following Colin to the kitchen.

"This looks like my apartment, so disorganized. I wish I could control my depression. I am so tired of taking drugs and other medications to help me."

Colin said.

"You just have too much clutter. You need to reorganize things."

Colin glanced at Joah. "I want to do it but refrain. It is like someone overweight who knows they should diet or exercise but refuse to do it and just ignore the situation."

"It is like this house. I could turn my back on it and forget about it, but I can't do it."

"Then you should purchase the house or try to get it."

"But I can't do repairs. It needs a lot of work, and what about furniture?"

"Joah, you are ignoring the situation. Didn't we just talk about this?"

"Yes, but this is a different situation."

"What is different about it? What is different about me and you? I have a depression problem and have to solve it and you have to find out why you are supposed to be in this house, what you are supposed to do, and then maybe we can find the answers."

Nodding my head without another thought, I was certain, "You are exactly right."

"Let's get the hell out of this house before we fall through the floor!" Colin commented.

We crawled through the window, closed and locked it, and climbed the ladder back to the beach. I turned to face the house; it did not look bad from afar. It was getting late, so Colin and I gathered our things and left the property.

I spent the next few days finalizing papers for the ownership of the house. There were a few problems, but I was given the key and permission to begin fixing the foundation. I packed up some tools, clothes, food, a sleeping bag, cooler, and a small tent and took a ferryboat to the premises. Though I was not certain why I was drawn to this place, it felt right. It felt like my place to be. It was beautiful waking up to the sounds of ocean waves, my front yard, and wild plants and tropical trees, my backyard. Most of my days were spent repairing the foundation by securing the wooden stilts and picking up branches, leaves, and garbage clinging to the supports. The floor seemed much more secure once I replaced the warped boards with new ones.

I looked at my watch; it was noon, and Colin usually came every other day on a taxi boat with supplies to the house. It circled the island every hour or so and dropped people off at different locations. A whistle blew and the ferryboat bobbed over waves to the shore. I helped Colin unload baskets of food, water, and building supplies.

Catching his breath, Colin chugged bottled water. "I hope you appreciate me coming to this place. I am getting sunburned," he said, ducking under the beach house.

"You don't have to go out of your way for me. The sun is not good for your pale skin," I told him, waving to the driver of the taxi as it spun away.

"I enjoy helping others," he said, wiping sweat from his brow.

"Why can't you be yourself? You always do things for others that you don't like to do, and you do nothing for yourself."

"I guess it is a part of my depression. I did go through a lot of my junk to eventually bring to this house when it is finished. I enjoy helping others. It makes me feel good about myself," he answered, sipping bottled water.

Grabbing a bottle of water, I sipped the cold liquid. "Looks like another scorcher," I said, looking up at the hot sun.

"I thought for sure you would return home by now."

I turned and answered smugly, "I am never going home. I love it here."

"Your family is not fond of your choice."

"I don't care. They are never happy about any of my choices."

"The house is decrepit and falling apart."

"It does not matter."

"It is not finalized yet. It could be taken away from you."

"The keys were given to me. That proves they are serious," I said, pounding a nail into a wooden support.

"Joah, your life has not been easy, and I don't want to see you lose everything."

"So what if I do. This has been the happiest time of my life," I told him, grabbing another nail.

"You can't take care of this place alone. You are not a carpenter."

"Not to worry. I know what I am doing."

Colin looked at me with concern. "Your family is very worried about you. They were devastated when you told them you were moving to an abandoned house in the middle of nowhere."

"I can manage on my own," I huffed.

"You need someone to be with you. It is not safe. And I am certainly not going to stay here with you," Colin said, tossing his arms into the air.

"I never asked you to stay. You would never be happy here. I could never handle the way you live in such disorganization."

"I live in depression and anxiety," he sighed.

"That is no excuse," I said, pushing away from him.

"You're really rude and inconsiderate; look how you treat me after coming all this way with supplies to help you."

"Get away from me!" I exclaimed, throwing my bottle of water against a wall and smacking a wooden post. "Why am I always the only one with faith?"

Colin jumped and spit dribbled down his chin. He grabbed his things, stammered and paced in the sand, and disappeared behind a dune.

I threw down the hammer, rebounded, and then ran after him screaming, "Damn you, damn you, you little shit, and what right do you have to tell me what to do? Huh, so tell me," I shouted, stammering and kicking my feet through the sand. Suddenly I felt very light-headed and nauseated, so I sat on a rock. I took a deep breath and slowly regained consciousness. I needed to get away and think. I changed into a swimsuit, packed some gear and water, and jogged along the shore. It was a picturesque run past dunes and beach grass, plush sandy hills and valleys, and it ended circling around a small island concealed in its own private foliage. Stopping and catching my breath, I placed my beach gear and towel on the beach. I removed my swimsuit and jumped into the ocean. It was cold and crisp, but once my naked body was submerged in the water, I was content and relaxed. A sudden wave caught me off guard and smacked me on the beach. Wiping my eyes and catching my breath, I sensed I was not alone. Standing naked in three feet of water, I noticed a stranger on the beach. I had never seen this guy before. Unaware of what to expect, I approached him with caution.

"I am sorry if I startled you," he said, holding a towel with closed eyes.

I grabbed the towel and flung it around my waist, "Who are you?"

He opened his eyes, smiled, and held out his hand, "Marshall, but call me Marsh."

"Why are you on this private beach?" I asked, tucking the towel.

"I did not see any signs that said 'private,'" he answered.

"No one ventures on these beaches. Do you live here?"

"No, I don't have any family; I'm a loner," he explained, turning away and returning to his duffle bag, tent, and backpack.

"Where are you from?"

"Nowhere," he answered, struggling with his gear. "I just thought that since I am alone and you are alone, you could use a friend."

I wondered, confused, "And what makes you think I am alone?"

"Why would you be swimming nude all by yourself if you had somebody else. I had seen you on the beach and feared revealing and introducing myself to you, but then I got brave enough to take a chance."

"It must have taken a lot of guts to face me," I said, pulling on my swimsuit.

Marsh scratched his shaved head. "I guess I got tired of being alone."

"And what brings you here? What do you want?"

"I don't know," he shrugged.

"Listen, I could use some help rebuilding a beach house. Can you help me?"

"Yes, I know a little about construction. What does it pay?"

"Not much—a place to live in the near future and some food."

"Sounds good, so when do we get started?"

"Just follow me," I said, helping him with his things. "By the way, I am Joah."

"Nice to meet you," Marsh answered, shaking my hand. "So how long have you lived on this beach?"

"'I have roamed these beaches since I was a child. I've even camped here, but this is the first time I have made a decision to live here."

"Where is the cottage or beach house?"

"It is just ahead," I pointed.

"How did you find it?"

"It found me. I was strolling along the beach during a storm and saw this abandoned beach house. I immediately knew I had to have it."

A sudden wave crashed on the shore as mist enveloped around us.

"Why was the house left abandoned?" Marsh inquired.

"Many years ago there was a hurricane and the people never came back. They are not sure if the owners died, but it is paid for, and no one has claimed it. The banks offered me a settlement that if I repaired it, I could live in it and eventually own it."

"Sounds like a good deal," Marsh answered, tugging at his gear.

We rounded a bend and the house stood directly in front of us. It still looked awry from the slanted supports. The railings were crooked, the steps cracked and splintered, and the walkway sagged on the right side. Many wild plants were overgrown and hanging across the warped roof. Standing beneath the house, I said, "What do you think?"

His mouth flew opened, shocked, and he backed away and ran across the beach.

"Marsh, wait," I begged, "it is not that bad." I chased him for a while, lost him, and then gave up. It was a very disheartening day. I struggled to be strong in my faith and prayed every day, but sometimes nothing seemed to turn out right. "Just run away and see what I think," I said, kicking my feet through mounds of sand.

One day while I was working on the house, a crackling noise echoed in the woods. Climbing down the ladder to investigate, I saw Colin with a basket, beach umbrella, and black bag. He brushed past me and dropped everything on the ground. "You look like you have seen a ghost," he observed, cracking open a can of soda and slurping it.

"I am just shocked to see you."

"You are really acting strange, and I can sense it."

I took a seat next to him. "I know my purpose in life."

"That's great," Colin answered, munching on a sandwich.

"I can help others to reach the other side of life without having to die."

Colin choked and guffawed.

"It is a special gift given to me."

"And you expect me to believe this?"

"I was hoping you would."

"That is insane!" Colin exclaimed. "Think about what you are saying. Would you believe me if I told you something as ludicrous as this."

"I thought for sure if anyone would understand it would be you. Maybe I can help you."

He jumped up, shoved everything into his black bag, and defended himself.

"Colin, please don't be angry with me. I am only trying to tell you what is going on with me," I explained, chasing him, but he took off running. I stopped and realized there was nothing I could do to bring him back. He had to come back on his own free will. Retreating to the beach house, I sat on the shore and finished my sandwich and soda. It was the fist time I had eaten in a while and didn't realize how hungry I was.

I was uncertain about my calling, this new challenge, and I didn't know if I was ready for all of the responsibility. A sudden noise startled me. Thinking it was Colin, I stood up to greet him.

Marsh stood in the brush with a towel. "I am tired of being naked and alone. Is the offer still standing?"

"Yes, it is," I laughed, shaking his hand and greeting him. "It is good to have you back."

Marsh looked directly at me. "You knew I was coming back, didn't you?"

"You have free will. I have no control over you."

"How do you support yourself?"

"I am a freelance writer. Mostly everything is given to me by others."

Marsh dropped his things on the shore and kicked through the sand. His feet moved so quickly that it looked like he was building a sand sculpture. "I must be honest with you. I have so many things to straighten out in my life that I have been running away for years."

"I am sure I can help you. How did you get into so much trouble?"

"The reason I ran away was not because of the house," he said, leaving his seat and pacing. "My life is very complex. I move from one place to the next, and I am tired of living in devastation."

I leaned against a chair and listened.

"I don't have much. I'm penniless, and a loser."

"Maybe it is time for you to change your life."

"I will only be a burden for you. I should leave."

"You just got here."

"You live in a condemned house. You have no furniture, no money, and neither do I. I have no right to be here."

"Marsh, I need your help and you need my help. At least you will have a foundation, somewhere to live, and we can rebuild this house."

He sat down and nodded. "Okay, let's see how this works out."

The next few weeks we worked on the foundation. We removed warped floor and deck boards and replaced them with new ones. It was also a lot of work removing the slanted supports, replacing them with larger ones, and securing them deeper into the sand. The roof leaked, so we removed mud and sand, leaves and broken branches, and old and rotted shingles. All of the debris was thrown into a hole we dug in the sand. New shingles were elevated to the top by a pulley, scattered around, and nailed to cover and replace the old ones.

The biggest problem facing me right now was the lack of food and supplies. Colin had not been to the beach house since our last fight. The coolers were empty, the wood and shingles were gone, and we were down to the last crusts of bread. Marsh and I planted some vegetable seeds, which were just starting to sprout, but they would not be ready for a month or longer. There was some vegetation on the island to eat, some orange and lemon trees, which were out of season, and some wild strawberries. Often we would go fishing on a small raft with poles and string, but neither of us had much luck and we hated cleaning dead fish. We often walked to the mainland for supplies and food, but my money was running out. I sat on the shore and looked out at the ocean.

"Time for a lunch break yet?" Marsh asked, rubbing his stomach. "I am starved."

"Me too," I said, unenthused.

"What is wrong?" Marsh inquired, sitting next to me.

"I am out of money, my parents won't give me any more, and I have not heard from my best friend, Colin, since our last fight."

"It is time I looked for a job," Marsh said. "We can't do much more on the house. I need money to pay my DUI, my bonds from jail, and other bills. You helped me with the paperwork and now I have to mail them out," he said, lighting up a cigarette.

"Where did you get the cigarettes?" I asked, watching him puffing.

"I traded with the islanders—trinkets, pens, lighters," he answered.

"Are you Trader Marn?" I asked, glaring at him.

"Yes, that is my island name."

"Yes, everyone from the mainland is talking about you and all of the treasures they have gotten from you."

Marsh took a puff of his cigarette and smiled. "I am the Marn man."

He smiled as wide a smile as I'd ever seen. Marsh was a good worker, but he often got on my nerves. He burnt food, placed too much wood on the campfire and almost burnt down the house, and this morning he slipped on tar and almost fell from the roof. His lack of concentration often troubled me.

"I am going to the mainland to look for a job. I am bored and hungry."

"Where will you go?"

"I don't know. I will find something," he answered, placing a few things into a small backpack.

"When will you be back?"

"Before nightfall," he answered, waving and leaving.

I sat on the shore and looked at my reflection in the water. My face was very dark from the sun, my hair lighter, and my beard thicker. Suddenly ripples formed over my face. At first I thought it was just waves, but suddenly it became heavier and more frequent. I jumped up and saw a small boat with supplies coming toward me. I was excited and could hardly control myself. As the boat neared the shore, I made out the appearance of Colin and his good friend Father Leonard. As soon as they reached the shore, I greeted them.

"Hello, Joah!" Father Leonard exclaimed, hugging me.

"It has been a long time."I replied, hugging him back

Colin walked past me and looked at the house. "Wow, you got a lot done," he observed, examining the new wooden supports.

"Yes, I met a guy on the shore, Marsh, and he has been helping me. We replaced the stilts, wooden floor boards, and most of the roof. He just left."

"It looks great, Joah," Father Leonard said, tugging on his gray beard.

"Do you know anything about this guy?" Colin asked.

"No, I just met him on the beach," I said, not telling him everything, since I knew Colin would not understand. I had to take my time with him.

"Well, Joah, I was told about your venture and took a collection from the parishioners of Saint John's Episcopal Church, and Colin and I bought some supplies and food for you."

"Thanks, Father and Colin, this will help me a lot."

"The food is not for your friend," Colin said.

"You have not even met this guy," I said, glaring at him. "Why are you judging him with such hostility?"

"You never told me anything about him."

"You weren't here."

"You couldn't call me or come visit me?" he asked, moving away.

"I was too busy working on the house."

"Joah, Colin did a lot of work to raise money for you. He talked to me about your future plans, and although I disagreed, he did not give up. I am going to start unloading all of the supplies. Go talk to him," Father Leonard said with a wink. I approached Colin and leaned on the railing. "What was I supposed to think? You took off without any explanation. I have not heard from you in two weeks."

Colin jumped at me clenching a fist. "I was rushed to the hospital thinking I had a heart attack, but it was only an anxiety attack. The entire time I was there I thought of you, my best friend, and where were you?"

"Colin, I am so sorry. I did not know," I apologized. "Why didn't someone tell me?"

"A telegram was sent to you. Didn't you get it?"

"No," I shrugged, "or else I would have gone straight to the hospital."

Colin recoiled and relaxed. "I hope you are telling the truth."

"Hey, thanks for the food and supplies. I really appreciate it."

Colin didn't answer and remained silent.

"I will talk to Marsh. Maybe he did not give me the telegram."

"You are welcome," he smiled. "The place looks great. You guys did a fantastic job."

"Thanks, Colin," I answered, hugging him. "It is so good to see you."

Colin backed away and leaned on a support, folding his arms and looking in the distance. "Have you sent anyone to the other side of life yet?"

"No, Marsh may be the first one."

Colin jumped as if he had just come out of a trance. He danced around in circles and stopped. "It took me a while to think through and analyze everything. I have known you for years and it has not been easy for me. It has been mainly you and I as friends, and it is difficult to see you with someone new."

"Colin, there will be many others. You are going to have to get used to it," I told him, approaching the ferryboat and unloading it.

"Why must it be like this?" Colin asked, grasping a bag of food.

"It is something that I must do to survive."

Colin nodded as we unloaded the boat, but I knew he did not understand. He had a faraway look on his face and remained silent. We unloaded wood, shingles, tools, and building supplies, and there was also a generator so we could now have light and work in the evening. It was battery operated, noisy, and spat and sputtered. Father Leonard showed me how to set it up, operate it, and use it to its fullest capacity. Colin was bored and tired and dropped on a blanket beneath the house and fell asleep.

"Please thank your parishioners for me. That was very kind of them," I said, stopping for a soda and facing Father Leonard.

"It was mainly because of Colin. He talked to me briefly about what you are doing. Though I don't understand, anything that is helping others to reach the Lord is worth it. When did you have this revelation?"

Suddenly I felt very weak and light-headed. My lungs seemed to collapse and block my breathing. I felt as though I was suffocating and drowning, but suddenly I breathed in fresh air and was okay. Sweat beaded on my brow and dripped down my face. A voice echoed in my brain, "Joah, Joah," and someone was shaking my shoulders. Everything was clear and focused back to reality. Father Leonard stood in shock beside me.

"Joah, what happened?"

Still in a daze, I wept. "Thank heavens Colin did not see this."

"Joah, what is wrong with you?"

Catching my breath, I dried my dripping face. "I don't know if Colin told you the entire story, but I had a dream and walked through it. It was the other side of life, and it is a beautiful, warm, and refreshing place. It is like love, Christmas, the ocean, the birth of a baby, and all of your most beautiful moments all in one. I cannot describe the feeling but have experienced it."

"And what does this have to do with what just happened?"

"I am ill and dying. The only way I can get my energy back is to help others to get to the other side of life," I said, nodding, still uncertain about this entire situation.

Father Leonard froze in amazement.

I finished my soda and looked out to sea. "Sometimes I awake and feel very lost. I sit in wonder and can't function. I don't want to face it."

"Does Colin know you are ill?"

"No, he knows nothing of my illness and only a little about my calling to help others leave this earth without having to die."

"Does your family or friends know anything?"

"No. Absolutely nothing."

"Why did you choose to tell me?"

"After my episode I had to tell you something. Maybe this was meant to be. I feel relieved now that I have told someone. It is a great burden from my shoulders."

There was a sudden grunting as Colin woke up, stretched, and yawned. "Sorry guys, I must have dozed off," he said, standing up.

"Now that we have unloaded everything, Colin awakes," I laughed.

"Hey, I helped a lot. The hot sun just tired me out."

"I appreciate everything you and Father Leonard have done for me. Thanks for taking time to help," I said, with sincerity and appreciation.

"It was a pleasure. So nice to see you," Father Leonard said, hugging me. When I looked into his large brown eyes, I could see worry and concern deep inside of him. Hoping to take it all away, I smiled from ear to ear to let him know that I was okay.

Colin and Father Leonard helped me get everything set up and organized. It was getting late, close to dusk, and they boarded the boat and left. I hugged them and waved to them until the ferryboat disappeared over the horizon. Suddenly I felt very lonely. I was used to having friends and family nearby. I looked around me and there was nothing but the chirps of birds, the wind, and the crashing of the waves onto the shore. I sat on the beach and watched the sun fade behind the clouds. A gust of wind made me shiver.

There was so much on my mind, so much to think about, and so many plans. I had to figure out how I was going to explain everything about myself to Marsh and how to explain the other side of life to him. How would he accept everything? What if he did not want to go? I needed help and was not ready to die.

"Joah, guess what," a voice echoed in the darkness.

I was startled and jumped.

"Sorry," he apologized, realizing he had scared me.

"No problem," I said, catching my breath.

"I just got a job at the small hospital on the island. It is nothing much, just taking care of patients, bathing them, and cleaning up their messes."

"That is great," I said, congratulating him.

"Where did all of the supplies come from?" Marsh asked, examining the new merchandise.

"My best friend Colin and Father Leonard took up a collection and brought the supplies here on a ferryboat. You just missed them."

"I would have liked to have met them," he said, checking out the generator. "Wow, we can have light."

"Yes, and we can work at night," I said, leaving the shore and joining him.

"I just hope this new job does not take up too much of my time so I can continue to help you."

"You need the money to pay off your debts."

Marsh danced around and looked at all of the new supplies. "There are new coolers, food, building supplies, tarps, blankets, shingles, wood. This may be enough to finish the house."

"Yes, I hope so," I said, leaning on the pile of wood.

Marsh looked into my eyes and stood next to me. "I have something to tell you."

"What is it?" I wondered.

"I have been following you for a long time. I watched you many times swimming in the nude. I was very attracted to you."

"I am not like that," I explained.

Marsh moved away from me and dug his feet into the sand. "I know. You are very gifted. I felt horrible and sacrilegious desiring sex from a prophet."

"I am not a prophet. Did you see me go through the Realm Incarnate?"

Marsh turned with tears in his eyes. "Yes, it was beautiful. It was the most overwhelming feeling I have ever experienced in all of my life."

"Why did you run away the first time I met you?"

Marsh stroked some of his facial hair and thought for a moment. "I was afraid of you and uncertain about leaving this earth, but then I made up my mind and came back."

"And what have you decided?"

It seemed like an eternity as I waited to hear his words. My heart was beating wildly and I was hardly breathing.

"I want to go. There is nothing for me here."

I took a deep breath and grasped his shoulder. "I think you have made the right decision. I will help you along the way. You must be free of debt before you can go and sign papers stating your decision."

"That will be no problem. Thanks for being so understanding," Marsh said, turning away from me.

"What is wrong?" I wondered, observing his reaction.

Marsh handed me a piece of parchment and moved away from me.

I unraveled the note and read it. "Why?" I asked.

Marsh danced around in circles, embarrassed, "First I forgot, and then I was jealous that you were receiving notes from other guys."

"How could you do this? Colin was very upset. He was in the hospital and I was not there for him."

"I don't blame you for being angry with me."

"Do you realize that thanks to him we have all of these supplies?" I said, glaring at him.

Marsh looked away from me. "I am aware of what I did wrong. You sound so much like my father, whom I hated. Look at the way my hair is growing in," he said, pointing to his hairline.

I looked at the top of his head and shrugged.

"I have the same receding hairline as he did. I need to cut my hair."

"What does this have to do with what we are talking about?"

"My father always made me feel stupid. I feel that way now. I don't mean to do thoughtless things; it just happens," he said, defending himself.

"We all make right and wrong decisions," I told him.

"Then I want to go to the other side of life to help myself," Marsh said, grabbing a hammer. "I want to help you finish this house before the monsoons."

"I appreciate all of your help."

"I promise I will never change my mind or turn away from you. I am sorry for not giving you the letter from Colin."

I smiled at him and grabbed something out of a box. "Before we continue with the house, I want to cut your hair. I have a pair of clippers." His entire face lit up. His eyes grew watery as he floated toward me and melted into a canvas chair. Marsh closed his eyes as I clipped off his hair, strand after strand, and the ocean waves rolled in and washed it all away.

Marsh and I worked most of the night. The new generator gave us extra light and we were able to do a lot of intricate things: connecting wires, plugs, and outlets; welding pipes and connectors together; and doing a lot of the woodwork around the windows and doors. It was amazing how much more we could do. There was also plenty to eat and drink, such as fruit, juice, milk, cookies, and chips. We drank and ate as we worked on the house. The new generated coolers kept everything cold and fresh. We both collapsed near dawn. We crept into our sleeping bags to hide from the morning chill.

Marsh leaned over and looked at me. "Thanks so much for cutting my hair. It means a lot to me. It is like shedding the hurt and pain that has been with me all of my life."

"It is a pleasure to help others like you," I shivered, trying to get warm.

Marsh thought for a moment and sniffled. "How will others find you?"

"How did you find me?"

"That is a good question," he answered. "I have been a wanderer all of my life until I came upon you."

I looked up at the starry sky. "Others will find their way here."

"What will you do for furniture?"

"Let's finish building the house and worry about that later."

Marsh fell asleep quickly. The sound of his voice turned into heavy breathing. The sounds of birds, animals, the ocean, and the wind took over. It seemed so loud as I drifted to sleep. I thanked God for all of the wondrous things that had occurred.

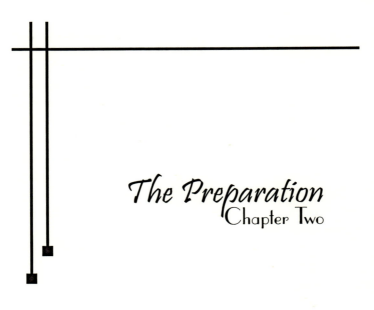

The Preparation
Chapter Two

IT WAS A VERY BUSY and challenging couple of weeks. Many brief storms and downpours kept us from working on the house. The winds and water constantly drenched the property, leaked into the house, and caused puddles and mud. Each day before we could start building and remodeling, we had to clean off the equipment, mop up the messes, and carry and move supplies over sludge and debris. The floors, windows, foundation, and roof were done. The wooden steps, deck, and railings were still crooked and shaky.

Marsh was working at the hospital and trying to make money to pay off his debts. I got all of his bills together, paid them with checks, and saved the receipts. I also tried to give him some extra money for helping me rebuild the house.

The blankets and sleeping bags, coolers, food and beverages, tools, and boxes of linens and drapes were taken into the house for safekeeping and to keep dry. We also loaded a ferryboat full of garbage, unwanted and unusable boards and scrap, and other trash to be taken to the mainland for disposal. It was a lot of work, but the house was finally shaping up.

Colin often came in the morning to help clean, decorate the walls, help put up draperies, and make the inside look livable. He often hid inside or beneath an umbrella to duck from the sun. Usually he left the premises after lunch.

"What do you think of the new pictures?" Colin asked, munching on some cookies.

"They look very nice. Thanks for taking time to frame them," I said, sitting in a canvas chair next to him.

"No problem. Most of them are taken from Broadway shows," he said, sipping on a cola.

"I know. I recognize some of the actors and actresses."

"Yes, several of them are from *Saturday Night Fever*, which we saw in New York," he said, wiping the sweat from his brow.

A wave crashed on the shore and the mist quenched our sweltering bodies. The refreshing coolness felt good. "Lots of humidity, but at least it is not raining," I said.

"Yes, it is nice to be outside for a change. It must be relaxing at night."

"Yes, Marsh and I often sit out here to enjoy the cool evening."

"I still have not met him," Colin said, shifting in his chair.

"He is only here in the evening. You know that. He works during the day to raise money to pay off all his debts so he can go to the other side of life. You can see him in the evening."

"Coming out here alone at night scares me."

"You could come and stay here for one night," I suggested.

"No, I have to take care of my cat. He freaks when I am gone too long. Doesn't Marsh have any obligations or family?"

"No, they are deceased. He is all alone."

He rolled his eyes and kicked his feet in the sand. "Is it legal for him to leave?"

"Yes, he has to sign papers allowing me to let him go, like a living will, and he leaves on his own free will."

"Why are you doing this? Isn't this time-consuming for you?" he asked, wondering.

"Yes, but it is very rewarding for me to help others," I said, reassuring him that this was something I liked to do.

"It still baffles me how this is helping you."

I shook my head in disgust. "Do I always have to have reasons for my actions?"

"Joah, you have always been someone who does sensible things. None of this makes any sense. You leave home to repair a decrepit house and help a complete stranger, and you are clueless as to why you are doing it. If I felt this was something that was helping you, I might feel differently," Colin said, grabbing his bag and beach umbrella.

I looked at Colin, thought of all of the things we had done together, our sincerity and honesty, and knew it was time to be truthful to him. Following behind him, I shuffled in front of him and glanced into his blue eyes. It was difficult for me to look directly at him. "You have done so much for me. Even though you don't understand what I am doing, you have accepted all of it. Not only that, you have helped me rebuild this house with contributions from the church. I want you to know how much I appreciate you."

A sudden smile lit up his face. "I enjoy doing things for you. You have also helped me a lot."

"Colin, you don't have to come out here so much. I know you have other obligations. I know you don't like the beach. You often do things for others just to fit in."

"I know. I just want to be part of everyone's life."

Large dark cumulus clouds hid the sun and produced darkness, but the sun peeked through them to bring back the light. I let its warmth play over my cold face. "Colin, the reason why I am here is because I am ill."

He stood in shock, unable to speak.

"I need to help others to the other side of life to regain strength and vitality. Each person who goes to the other side of life will help me get better," I said, walking beside him.

"Jesus, I don't know what to say. When did you find this out?" He stopped walking.

"It occurred a few months ago. I was feeling very tired and weak. I went to the doctors and they said I was deteriorating inside like an old man. I went through the Realm Incarnate and I regained my strength. As soon as I returned, I began feeling the same aches and pains."

Colin continued walking ahead. "I don't know what I would do if I lost you as a friend. Maybe I can help you find others to go to the other side of life. I feel so awful not believing you."

"It is something I don't understand myself," I told him.

"I would even be willing to go to the other side of life if it would help you stay alive. You have so much more to give. I live on welfare because of my depression and anxiety. How am I helping others?" he shrugged, leading the way across the dunes.

"Colin, I really appreciate your thoughtfulness and willingness to go, but I need you here. All I ask of you is to be strong for me."

He stopped at the wooden walkway leading to the mainland and hugged me. "I will do my best. Thanks so much for telling me. It is getting dark and I need to return home. It all makes so much sense now," he said, waving and disappearing behind a grove of palm trees.

An abrupt breeze brushed across my shoulders and made me shiver. I was not fond of my life or ready to face reality. It was not easy for me to accept my calling. I wanted so much to be normal, just a regular guy, and to have a wife and family. I dreamt of being married with children and having a nice house and a good job in the city. Loneliness seemed to cover me as I walked back home. I lived on an island away from civilization in a decrepit house with no money or job, living by faith and hope to help others to the other side of life. This was not what I had planned for my life. It did not take long to get back home. I sat on the beach and watched the sun fading over the horizon as nighttime arrived.

I grasped a notebook and wrote down my thoughts and feelings. Often when I was feeling sorry for myself, it would help to jot things down on paper. This was my way of hiding from reality. Instead of drinking or taking drugs, my escape was my writing.

"What are you doing out here alone?" a voice echoed behind me. I turned my head to see Marsh puffing on a cigarette. Inviting him to sit with me, I said, "Did you get done early from work?"

"Yes," he answered, pulling up a chair. "It's going to be a chilly evening; already there is a chill in the air."

"Yes, I should build a fire. I was not expecting you until later."

Marsh sucked on his cigarette. "I hate that hospital; I'm tired of cleaning up shit from those ungrateful people. How much more money do I need to finish paying off all of my debts? I also noticed that you have been sick the last couple of days. I don't want to see you die before I go to the other side."

"Your debts should be paid off within a month. I am not going anywhere."

"Damn, I am so sick of that senior home. I was thinking of maybe just working at a fast-food restaurant, a pizza place. An internet cafe with hoagie sandwiches is opening, and I was also thinking of working there," he said, crushing his cigarette in the sand.

"But the hospital is paying you so well."

"Yes, but I hate each day that I am working there," he said, fidgeting, looking for food.

"Are you hungry?"

"Yes, starved," he answered, "and plus I can get free meals working at the cafe."

"That is your decision," I said, leaving the beach and gathering wood for a fire.

"I met a woman at the hospital, a remarkable lady, and she comes every day to see her husband. He had a stroke a year ago. He does not talk, move, eat, or swallow; he is like a vegetable. She exercises him, cleans up his mucous, talks to him, dresses him, and never gives up hope."

"Wow, she sounds like a saint," I said, starting the fire with kindling and getting the wood to catch.

"Well, her husband had to be put on a hospice program and died a week ago. She is very lonely and depressed. I think she would like to leave this world and go to the other side of life. She misses her husband very much."

Tossing some burgers on a pan and opening a can of beans, I started cooking the food. "Have you mentioned anything about me to her?"

"No, I wanted to talk to you first," Marsh said, sitting on a canvas chair next to the fire.

"Yes, you could invite her to the house," I said, flipping the burgers.

"She also wants to sell her house and get rid of all of her furniture."

"Maybe she has family to give it to."

Marsh jumped up excitedly. "Her family took what they wanted and there is a lot left."

"Great. I could use the furniture," I said, serving the food on a plate.

Marsh looked at me with concern. "I saw you the other night choking and coughing, struggling to catch your breath, and you scare me. You need to get me and this woman to the other side of life. You need strength to survive. The world needs you to help others, and there is no need for me to be here."

"What is the woman's name?" I inquired, munching.

"They call her Mum."

"Let me know when she can come and talk to me."

"That will be fine," Marsh said, finishing his sandwich and beans.

I finished my food and began cleaning up the plates and glasses.

"Joah, why you?" Marsh asked, glancing at me.

"What do you mean?" I asked, not understanding.

"You are one of the nicest guys I have ever met in my life. You should have a wonderful life with a family and wife, yet you live on this island away from others, ill, and have to depend on others to make you well."

I sat near the fire and thought about his words.

Tears welled in his eyes as he spoke. "And here I am, a screwup with so many psychological problems and dependencies, a failure with a horrible family. I have no one; I'm all alone. Why does it have to be this way?"

Thinking about his hurt and anxiety, I answered, "Without someone like you, I would die, so there is a reason for you. Don't be so hard on yourself."

"I just feel so helpless. Will God forgive me for all of my mistakes?"

"Yes, you have redeemed yourself and that is your reason for being here with me—you are preparing yourself for the hereafter. You have also been a great help with this house."

"I am really going to miss you. As much as I would like to stay, I know that going to the other side of life will help me and help you."

Nodding, I was lost for words.

"Thanks for this wonderful experience," he said, leaving the fire and going to bed.

Sitting next to the fire and enjoying its warmth, I wondered what the next few days would be like, what experiences would unfold, and how to handle them. I was scared. There were so many other strong religious leaders who should have been chosen for this task. I was just a writer for a newspaper, a boy-next-door type, and there was nothing special or different about me. I did not tell my friends, but I was also afraid of dying before I was able to help them. My illness seemed to be getting worse and the pains were increasing. I tried to hide my fears from them.

I stood up and put another log on the fire. The warmth felt invigorating. I munched on a burger and beans, sipped a can of soda, and enjoyed my dinner. I did not realize how hungry I was. Glancing at the reflection of the fire against the house, I was proud of my accomplishment. I had helped my father with household chores, but I never thought I could rebuild an entire house. I had discovered so much about myself. There were so many talents hidden deep inside of me that remained closed, and now they were opened. I finished my meal, washed the plates, and cleaned up the premises.

I retreated to my sleeping bag, leaned my head against the pillow, and looked up at the sky. It was a beautiful starlit night and the moon was bright and full. Tomorrow I was going to start carrying things into the house and setting up household. I was grateful for the movie-star pictures, ocean-scene pictures, and art work Colin had framed, displayed, and hung on the walls. He did his part to make known his acceptance of the new place. It made me happy that he gave his approval. I closed my eyes and fell asleep.

Rays of sun played off my face and I awoke to the smell of fresh coffee. Marsh's rushing around, showering, and cooking breakfast startled me. I opened my eyes, stretched, and sat up.

"Would you like some breakfast?" Marsh asked, scrambling some eggs.

"Sure, sounds good," I answered, accepting a cup of coffee from him.

Tossing potatoes on a pan and cooking some eggs, he handed me a plate.

"Looks good," I said, as he filled my plate with food.

Marsh dug into his food, sipped his coffee, and sat in the sand across from me. "I wonder sometimes what it will be like on the other side."

"I really don't know," I commented, dodging his glance.

"I think you do know. When did you first become ill?"

I sipped my coffee, choked, and answered, "I don't know. Where does bad health come from? Germs, genetics, and who knows."

"Were you ill before you came back from the Realm Incarnate?"

"The illness did occur around that time," I answered abruptly.

"So maybe you crossed the line and went somewhere you were not supposed to be by mistake. Maybe this is your punishment."

"Stop it! Quit trying to analyze everything. I have enough to think about. All I can tell you is that this is my calling on this earth. I have been chosen to help others reach the other side of life," I answered, finishing the food and throwing my plate against a wall.

"I am sorry. I did not mean to upset you."

"I don't want to talk about this right now," I answered, sipping the coffee.

"I understand. I just want to be sure of where I am going."

"All I can tell you is it is like nothing you have ever felt or experienced before in your life. It's something that steals your breath away and leaves you in awe. A warmth more beautiful than love fills you with peace."

"Sounds wonderful." he said, finishing his food and coffee.

"Thanks for the coffee and breakfast. I will clean up the plates."

"Thanks. See you later," he waved, munching on a piece of toast.

I got out of bed, folded the blankets and sheets, and washed the cups and plates. Unloading boxes of plates, cups, and kitchen utensils, I began finding places for everything in cabinets and on shelves. Around late afternoon, music and voices echoed along the shore. Stepping to the deck and looking across the bay, I saw a ferryboat with balloons docked on the shore. I raced down the stairs and ran across the beach. My mother and father. Colin, and Father Leonard stepped from the ramp to the beach. I greeted each of them, shook hands, and was so overwhelmed to see everyone.

"Happy birthday!" everyone exclaimed, smiling and laughing.

Tears rolled down my cheeks. I remember when I was younger and how much my birthdays meant to me, but now they were not important. Birthday? I was so busy working on the house, thinking about other things, that the days and months were just passing before me. "Thanks," I said with joy and gratitude for everyone.

Dad walked toward the house and looked around the area.

Colin and Father Leonard walked away and began unloading more supplies.

Mom grabbed my arm and looked at me. "You look much thinner, but your tan looks great," she commented, examining me.

"I have been eating, but I've been burning it all off from working on the house and swimming."

"Son, don't you miss writing and working as a journalist?" she inquired, pushing her curly salt-and-pepper hair away from her face.

"No, it was not rewarding for me."

"And living like this is?" she commented, twisting and turning her thin body, pointing to the surrounding area.

"Mom, I love it here. I have never felt so happy and alive and fulfilled. I write every day."

"Don't you get lonely out here?" she asked, glancing at me with her green eyes.

Thinking about her question, I nodded, "Everyone gets lonely at certain times, whether you have someone or not, and you just accept it and go on with your life."

"I know you have a stranger living with you. How do you know you can trust him? Isn't it dangerous just to let a complete stranger live with you?"

"Marsh is a nice guy. I trust him," I answered, feeling very aggravated.

"Joah, this is not like you," she said, very concerned.

"Then maybe you never really knew me, because this is me," I answered, pushing her away and joining Dad. His eyes were glued to the roof and gutters, and he moved around examining them. I stood beside him with my head in the air. Following my dad like a puppet, I said, "What do you think of the house?"

"Not bad," he said, tossing his receding gray hair. "Colin showed me a picture of it a few days ago. I am impressed. It looks great, but the gutters are split and rotting and need replaced. I brought some new ones with me."

"Sounds like a good idea."

"Yes, I got them for a good price. If you don't change them, the rainwater could overflow and cause leaks in your roof."

"Thanks, Dad," I replied, grasping his large shoulder.

"I can't climb a ladder, but I can tell you what to do. Most of the pieces are put together already."

"Great, I will help unload the pieces. Will we be done before nightfall?"

"Oh, definitely," he told me.

Colin, Father Leonard, and my dad helped me unload the gutters. I attached the ladder to the side of the house and began ripping the old ones from the side of the house and replacing them with new gutters. I did not like heights or hanging on a ladder, but just being with my dad and working with him made the fear drift away. I could see everything: Mom and Colin were relaxing on the shore beneath an umbrella, Father Leonard was unloading gutter pieces from the boat, and Dad was helping me and telling me what to do. The wind, mist from the ocean, and the pounding waves surrounded me. It was the perfect day. It did not take long to attach the hinges, nails, and screws. It was close to dusk, the project was complete, and it was time for dinner.

Father Leonard cooked some burgers and hot dogs, Mom made some potato salad, and Dad made his famous baked beans with spices, tomatoes, and brown sugar. It all smelt very good.

Colin sat alone on the shore beneath an umbrella. A smile covered his face from ear to ear and he looked like he was in a trance. It was the first time I recalled seeing him so peaceful. I sat next to him and wanted to be a part of his dream. His blue eyes drifted over me. "I can see why you love it here so much. I have never taken time to relax and enjoy the beauty of the ocean."

"Yes, we often are so busy with our own lives, we fail to recognize the beauty surrounding us."

"Joah, you have to talk to your mom and help her understand what is going on with you."

"Must you spoil the moment," I said, glancing at the ocean.

"Joah, she loves you and is concerned about your future."

"I know. I will talk to her before she leaves," I said. "So the ocean has lured you into its grasp."

"Yes, the wind, the mist, the salty smell, the never-ending feeling of eternity, the unexplained—it is all out there somewhere."

"That is only a glimpse of the way I felt in the Realm Incarnate."

"Wow, I cannot imagine anything like it. The feeling of love, compassion, and the unknown; it takes my breath away."

"You are hooked," I laughed.

Colin and I left the shore and joined the others at the picnic table where we sat and ate the scrumptious food. It was such a pleasure to eat someone else's cooking besides my own. After the dishes were cleared and washed, a huge cake with candles appeared and everyone sang happy birthday to me. It felt good to be remembered.

Munching on the cake, I turned my head and Marsh appeared. I took him around and introduced him to my family and friends. It was a joyous occasion and everyone laughed and enjoyed the party. The evening grew chilly and a nice bonfire warmed the night. Everyone sat around it and talked. Mom, Marsh, and I left the others and strolled along the shore. It was the perfect evening for a walk.

The waves pounded on the shore and sprayed a mist over us. There were sounds of birds, animals, and other creatures stirring along the dunes. I was startled and jumped, not because of them, but because of my mom and her thoughts. I did not want to face her, look at her, or tell her the truth. My biggest fear was how she would accept everything.

"So how did you and my son meet?" Mom inquired, arms folded around her from the chill.

Marsh looked at me for an answer.

"We met on the beach," I said, looking at Mom. "I was swimming naked and he saw me."

"What?" she answered in shock. "Why?"

"I like the feel of the ocean water against my naked body."

"Was Marsh naked too?"

"No, he was wandering in the dunes and needed a friend. It took a lot of guts for him to introduce himself."

"Couldn't he come at a better moment?" she wondered.

"Is there such a thing? You have got to take the risk or chance whenever you can. This was Marsh's time," I told her with compassion.

"And what is this Realm Incarnate that you have spoken to me and your father about? Marsh, are you sure about going?"

Marsh flung a look at me and I nodded for him to continue.

"Yes, Mrs. Sloan. It took a lot of soul-searching and thinking, and I am sure. I have messed up my life and Joah is helping me get myself back on track. I don't have anyone else worthwhile in my life. I have been nothing but a failure and I hope things are better on the other side."

Mom grabbed my arm and sighed. "Why does it have to be you? Can't someone else do this?"

"This has been a rewarding experience for me and it is something I have to do for survival."

"I don't understand," she said, looking at both of us.

The sound of the ocean seemed so loud, an echo chamber, and it was making me deaf. My hearing returned as I spoke, "I need to do this to feel better."

"What is wrong with you?"

"Mom, I am ill."

"How did this happen?"

"It began around the time I first went through the Realm Incarnate."

"Maybe it was wrong of you to go through it, just like we are not supposed to mess around with death or the hereafter."

I thought about what my mom said, thinking about all I was going through, all of my experiences, and I had no regrets. "Mom, it has been the most wonderful time of my life. Visiting the hereafter was one of the most overwhelming experiences of my life. I felt no wrong or sorrow, just joy, happiness, and peace."

"If it is all so grand and right and pure, then why are you sick?"

We turned around and began walking back to the house. A sudden breeze brushed over the palm trees, the branches rustled, and debree fell over us.

"I don't know," I shrugged. "Maybe this is something that has been with me for a long time and has gotten worse."

"Son, how ill are you?"

Sweat beaded my forehead and I shivered. "It comes and goes. Sometimes I am fine, sometimes weak and weary. I become breathless and nauseated, I feel faint, and pain runs through my body, but then it disappears and I am fine."

"How do you know that sending someone to the other side will help you?"

"When I was in the Realm Incarnate, I felt healed, strong, and alive, and I had no recollection of the pain."

"So each person that leaves this earth will make you better."

"Yes, exactly," I nodded, reassuring her.

Mom turned toward Marsh and smiled. "Thanks for helping my son. I know this must not be easy for you. I am glad he has you as a friend to help him with the house. It looks great and this is a beautiful island. Maybe I will come and live here with you."

"Oh, no, you won't," we both replied.

The smell of the campfire filled our lungs as we neared the house. We joined the others, who were talking and laughing. The night came to an end and everyone began packing up things and getting ready to leave. We hugged and extended our farewells and loaded on the boat. It was a very rewarding evening, a great birthday, and everyone seemed content and happy. Colin decided to stay since he had work to do on some of his photos and frames and also because it was a long way to his home from the boat docks. Everyone waved as the ferryboat left and disappeared across the horizon. Marsh walked back to the house.

"I am honored that you have decided to stay," I said, turning to Colin.

He looked away from me and kicked the sand. "Are you really?"

His answer caught me off guard. "Yes, I have wanted you to stay for a while. You know that."

"So why did you go for a walk with Marsh and your mom instead of me?"

"Mom knows you, but she has never met Marsh."

"What does that have to do with anything?"

His question made me think. I paused. "I wanted to explain to Mom about my illness and to let her meet the guy who was going to the other side."

"So is he more important than I am?"

I knew Colin well and I had to handle this with sensitivity and clear thought. "I just think you are not used to having someone else in my life. He is important to me now because I am helping him to reach the other side. He can never take your place. You will always be my best friend. That will never change. Once he leaves, he can never return. You will always be here."

Colin seemed more relaxed and smiled. "I just don't want to lose you as a friend."

"That will never happen," I reassured him, sitting next to the fire. We talked for a while, ate some leftover birthday cake, and enjoyed the pleasant evening. It was getting late. Marsh was fast asleep beneath the deck. I got some plastic and two sleeping bags and set everything up next to the fire. Our conversation faded as we got tucked in and comfortable, and we fell asleep.

Colin was startled by water and splashing footsteps and opened his eyes. He unzipped the sleeping bag, stretched and yawned, and was startled by noise and footsteps.

"Would you like a fresh cup of coffee?" Marsh asked.

Colin accepted the cup and sipped the hot liquid.

Marsh continued to get ready.

Colin left the sleeping bag, tugged on his boxer shorts, and walked toward Marsh. He felt very uncomfortable and scared, but he wanted to meet him. Dodging his glance, he muttered, "Hey, I am Colin."

"Yes, Joah has told me a lot about you," he said, shaking his hand.

"Same here," Colin replied, sipping his coffee.

Marsh brushed his teeth, placed shaving lather on his face, and continued to get ready for work.

"How do you like your job?"

Glancing at his face in a mirror, he retorted, "I hate it! I am so tired of cleaning up piss and shit. As it gets closer to my time to work, I get more and more frustrated."

"Why do you do it?" Colin asked, shuddering.

He lit up a cigarette and puffed. "To get out of this horrible life, to help Joah get better, and to pay off my debts. I have made a lot of mistakes in my life and I am struggling to redeem myself."

"How did you meet Joah?"

Marsh paced around the deck and glared at him. "I was attracted to his hot and sexy body. I saw him swimming naked and wanted him. I was very jealous of you," Marsh said, shaking the cigarette in his fingers. He walked in circles and stopped. "It was very wrong of me, lustful, and I feel awful about my evil thoughts," he turned, facing Colin.

"Why were you jealous of me?" he wondered.

"I thought there was something going on between the two of you," he answered, turning away, puffing. "I did a horrible thing. I am always doing stupid things."

"You are a very scary character," Colin told him.

"I know," he answered, crushing his cigarette into the sand. "I hid the letter that you sent to him about you being ill. It was my fault he did not come to see you," Marsh told him, buttoning his shirt.

Colin jumped up and flung a fist at him. "That was really an awful thing to do."

Marsh blocked his punch. "Please don't hate me. Don't start a scene; I don't want to alarm Joah. Just forgive me. I need your forgiveness to go to the other side. I can't leave any stone unturned."

Colin calmed down and lowered his arm. "You don't deserve to go to the other side or to have a great friend like Joah."

Marsh's eyes grew watery as he faced Colin. "I know I don't. He has been a great inspiration to me. Promise me that you will always be kind and thoughtful to him, not like me. You have one over me."

"What is that?" Colin inquired.

"You will be with him to see others reach the other side. I will be gone," he answered, waving and leaving for work.

Colin stood in amazement, unable to speak or move, and his entire body felt numb and rigid. He grabbed his umbrella, walked to the beach, and listened to the waves. It took a while before the sun reached him, thawed him out, and made him come back to life. Each day he was more amazed by the beauty of the ocean.

"Can't get away from it, can you?" I said, handing Colin a cup of coffee.

Colin jumped and was startled by my appearance "Hey, Joah! It has taken me in its grasp," he replied, accepting the coffee.

"What time did you awake?" I yawned, sitting.

"Early, Marsh startled me."

"Yes, he is noisy," I said, sipping the coffee.

Colin faced me and looked into my eyes. "I am so sorry for blaming you for not coming to see me. It was not your fault."

"I take it you talked to Marsh."

"Yes, there are things I like about him and hate about him."

"Yes, I know what you mean," I chuckled.

A sudden breeze brushed through the palm trees and dry leaves scattered around us.

"I can understand his jealousy and why he did not give you my note, but why are you helping a gay man?"

I sipped the coffee and shrugged. "It does not matter to me what you are, but what is in your heart."

"Doesn't it bother you being with him, sleeping near him, thinking that he might try something with you? It would bother me."

I stood up and looked out at the ocean. "I had a long talk with him. He told me how he felt, and I made it clear to him that I am straight. I trust him."

"Joah, it makes me feel yucky. Does he think I am gay?"

"No, he has not mentioned anything about it," I said, reassuring him.

"How can you live with someone like him—negative attitude, smoking, swearing? He scares me."

I tossed a stone into the ocean. "He has had a horrible life; he lost his family at an early age. I believe if he would have had someone who cared, he could have been a different person."

Colin grabbed his towel, umbrella, and black bag. "And why didn't you tell me the truth?"

I kicked sand along the beach, thought for a moment, and answered. "I did try, but you would not listen. I didn't know what happened to the message until days later, and also I did not want you to be angry at Marsh."

Colin nodded. "I can understand that," he answered, handing me his cup. "It is about time for me to go."

"I am so glad you stayed the night. You are always welcome here."

"Each time I come here, I learn more," he answered, waving, following a path that led to the mainland.

Entering into the house and looking around, I saw contributions from everyone. Mom had helped with the kitchen, Dad had helped with the roof gutters, Father Leonard had brought supplies, Marsh had dedicated his time and effort to rebuilding, and Colin had donated his art work and pictures. All the rooms needed was furniture to make them complete.

I was feeling weak, light-headed, and unbalanced and rested inside the house late into the afternoon. This attack was horrible and it scared me. I felt faint, coughed and choked, and blacked out. Sweat beaded my forehead, dribbled down my brows and lashes, and burnt my eyes. I regained consciousness, opened my eyes, and struggled to breathe. Voices echoed outside. I recognized one of them to be Marsh. The second one was unfamiliar to me, and it was a woman's voice. I stood up, stumbled, and entered onto the deck. I grasped the railing for support as my strength returned to me. Turning to face them, I smiled and waved.

"Hello, this is Brianne Slinsky, Mum, and she is the woman I told you about."

"Oh, yes, how nice to meet you," I said, wondering who she was.

"Hello," she muttered, lightly shaking my hand. She turned away from me and looked over the railing. "What a beautiful view of the ocean," she said, letting the breeze brush through her curly gray hair.

"Yes, I really like it here. Marsh has helped me rebuild the place."

"I really don't know why I am here," she stuttered, facing me.

"Then why did you come?"

She avoided the question and looked through the sliding door. "Why do you live in a house without furniture?"

"I am working on it," I told her.

"I am just very sad and needed to get out," she said, sitting on a canvas chair.

Suddenly it was clear to me who Mum was—the older woman who lost her husband, the one Marsh had informed me about. This could be a new person to go to the other side of life.

Marsh sat next to her and placed an afghan over her legs. "Mum gets cold very quickly."

"Yes," she said, snuggling under the material.

"I am so glad you came to visit me."

"Yes, I can't stay very long. I don't like walking at night."

"I can understand that," I said, touching her shoulder.

"I am sure Marsh has told you about me. My husband and I were together for over fifty years. I hate being alone."

"She went every day to visit her husband. He lost his speech years ago the day after Mother's Day."

"Enough of this! How can you help me?"

Her quick response caught me off guard. I was not finished with Marsh, uncertain about his outcome to the other side, yet I wanted to build up her faith in me without losing her. Unsure or uncertain of how to answer her, I said, "My heart is dedicated to others suffering in pain and I want to make them better."

She hesitated to answer. "How can you do that?" she wondered.

"It is a long story. I can meet you for lunch and explain to you what I can do to help you."

"That sounds nice," she nodded, grasping the afghan.

Marsh stood up and helped her out of her chair. "I am going to escort her home. I will see you in a short while."

"Sounds good," I said, following them down the wooden stairs to the ground.

"There is something very mystical and special about you," Mum observed, looking into my eyes.

I stood amazed and lost for words.

"Meet me tomorrow at the Mainland Cafe for lunch, noon?"

"I will look forward to it," I said, nodding, smiling.

"Great, let's go," she said, pointing ahead of them, grasping Marsh's arm.

"See you later," Marsh said, waving.

"Be careful. It will be dark soon," I said, watching them until they faded behind the dunes. It was not long before the sun faded behind the ocean and cast a beautiful sunset over the horizon. I watched it until darkness covered the land. Night critters began chirping and chanting in the shrubs and wild grasses. I built a fire for warmth and sat on the beach. There were so many uncertain things on my mind. Sometimes I did not like being alone and thought too deeply. Although a lot had been accomplished, there was a long way to go. My concentration was disturbed by something jumping out of the brush. I thought it was a wild animal, but it was just Marsh.

"Looks like you just saw a ghost," Marsh said, joining me by the fire.

"Can't you enter without scaring me, like a normal person?" I jumped.

"Sorry about that," he answered, puffing on a cigarette.

I stared at Marsh. "You are my first victim to send to the other side."

The fire sparked and hissed. "Yes, that is true."

"Marsh, what if I am wrong and don't have the powers?"

"Joah, you are scaring me," he answered, tossing his cigarette into the fire. "I hope I have not redeemed myself for nothing."

"Why must you always think of yourself? What about me?" I demanded.

"Where did this fear come from?

"This is my first time. This is all new for me," I answered, rearranging the sparking logs on the fire.

"You must have faith. I have faith in you. I am ready to go," Marsh replied.

I glanced into Marsh's eyes, "Maybe that is a part of it. I have worked with you and grown with you and now I have to let you go. It is not easy for me."

"I know how you feel. I tend to grow close to others and miss them when they leave or die. Will you miss me?"

His question caught me off guard, surprised me, but it was one of my fears and he sensed it. "Yes, you have been such a big help."

"Joah, this is your goal as a mediator. I will miss you too."

"I know I must let you go, yet it is not easy to do. I have grown close to you. It is not easy for me to trust someone."

"You must make new friends, help others to reach the other side, and keep that as your main goal."

I looked up from the fire and smiled. "Thanks. Your hard work and strength has been a great inspiration to me."

"I have never been close to anyone. I've only had one-night stands, But you have proved to me that there are genuine people in the world. I would like to go through the Realm Incarnate Friday. I am ready."

It was not going to be easy for me to lose Marsh. "That will be fine," I answered, watching the fire glow over his face.

"What did you think of Mum?" he asked, sitting on a canvas chair.

"She seems very perceptive, knowledgeable, and nice."

"Yes, she deserves to leave the earth and be with her husband. I think she will be a good friend for you."

"I am sure she will," I answered, looking at him from across the fire.

"Well, I am getting tired. I need to get a good night's rest before my departure. Is everything taken care of for me?"

"Yes, you have redeemed yourself, your bills are finished, and you are ready to go."

"Good. I would like to go on Friday, two days from today, late in the afternoon," he yawned, retreating to his sleeping bag.

"That will be fine. I am eager to talk to Mum and get to know her," I answered, looking over at Marsh. He was asleep and snoring. My deepest fear was loneliness. I did not like the nights being away from my friends and family. Soon Marsh would be gone and I was not certain if Mum would want to stay with me since she had plans all ready about staying at the same nursing home where her husband once had resided. I sat by the fire, nestled in its warmth, and it took the chill from my body. I was feeling much better, no relapses, and I knew that letting Marsh go would help me even more. The fire grew dim. Weariness took over me and I snuggled into my sleeping bag and fell asleep.

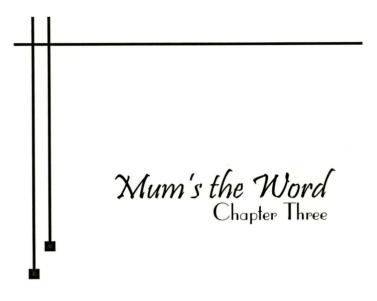

Mum's the Word
Chapter Three

I AWOKE LATE AND BEGAN rushing to get ready. I had not gone out to lunch with anyone for a long time. I trimmed my hair, side burns, moustache, and goatee. I could not pick out anything to wear—shorts, jeans, a T-shirt, or shirt, and I rummaged through my clothes uncertain about how to dress.

Marsh was up early and finished some carpentry work in the kitchen. He packed all of his old clothes in boxes to take to Goodwill. He did not have many valuables, jewelry, or expensive items, but he did not want to leave his junk for me to clean up.

I picked out an outfit for Marsh to wear to the other side and he helped me pick something nice to wear to the luncheon with Mum. It was a dark-blue shirt, a light-blue tank top beneath it, and baggy jean shorts. It was casual, neat, and clean looking. I was happy with it as I left the house and walked to the mainland. It was a hot and muggy day, cloudy and no breeze, and it looked like it was going to storm. Once I got to the mainland, it cleared and the sun peeked through the clouds. I climbed the wooden steps to the Mainland Cafe, walked through the front door to the lobby, and looked for Mum.

"May I help you?" a hostess asked, clutching a menu.

"Yes, I am waiting to meet a woman. Is there anyone waiting for someone?"

Suddenly a pleasant voice sounded behind me. Mum grasped my arm. "Nice to see you, Joah," she said, kissing my cheek.

"Nice to see you too," I answered, turning my head toward the hostess. "My guest is here."

She smiled and showed us to a table looking out at the ocean.

"This is very nice," Mum said, scooting into the booth.

"Yes, it is," I agreed, sitting across from her.

"Nice view of the ocean," she observed.

"Yes, it is very pleasant. Good choice."

The hostess handed us menus. Mum and I opened them and looked through the items. There was a nice selection of sandwiches, salads, soups, and pastas.

"Would you like something to drink?" the waitress asked, also suggesting a few appetizers and specials.

"Hot tea," Mum said.

"Just water with lemon," I answered.

"Do you need a few minutes to order?"

"Yes, give us a chance to look at the menu," Mum said, ushering her away.

"What looks good to you?" I asked.

"Just don't seem to have an appetite," she answered. "Ever since my husband past away, I have no enthusiasm for life."

"I can imagine how you feel. It is difficult to lose Marsh, and I have only known him for a few months."

"Try fifty-plus years," she huffed, with watery eyes.

"That is why I am here to help you."

She recoiled and lifted her shoulders. "What can you do?"

"I can help you to go to the other side without having to die."

She guffawed and grinned. "I will believe it when I see it."

The waitress returned with our drinks, took our orders, and walked away.

"You can come and watch Marsh leave tomorrow. He is my first one. Father Leonard is giving him his last rites. A few friends will be at my place to see him go."

She plopped a tea bag into an urn and swirled it around. "How did you get these powers? It just seems too good to be true."

"First of all you have to redeem yourself, have your life totally together, and if not, I won't be able to help you."

"Why do you want to do this? You have your entire life ahead of you and you should be enjoying your youth."

I took a sip of my water, nodded, and glanced at her. "I am ill. Each person I send to the other side will help my health. If I can help you, then you can help me."

"How did this happen?" she inquired, pouring the hot brew into her cup.

I took a few moments to gather my thoughts and replied. "I stumbled across the Realm Incarnate, the entrance to the other side. I have always been very inquisitive. Sometimes I think that being ill is my punishment for venturing into something secretive and not allowed. I played with the hereafter."

"Do you have a disease?"

"No, I got checked by a doctor and it is just a deterioration of the body. I can't stop it. I often get light-headed, weak, and nauseated and struggle to regain my strength."

The waitress brought our lunches. We both ordered grilled chicken salads, and began eating.

"Is there a name for it?" she asked, munching on her salad.

"No, and the doctor has never seen anything like it."

"That is a shame that a young guy like you has to suffer so much."

"You could make my suffering less by coming to Marsh's going-away party," I suggested, thinking this would be a good way to show her how the Realm Incarnate works. I waited with anticipation, wondering what she thought. It seemed like an eternity until she finally responded.

"I would like to be there for Marsh. He is a very nice guy, odd and different, but I know he deserves to be in a better place. He has redeemed himself. They all loved him at the senior home," she said, sipping her tea.

"I am happy to hear that," I breathed, relieved she was coming tomorrow.

"Would you like me to come and get you tomorrow?" I asked, finishing my salad.

"No, I will come on the ferryboat. I will definitely be there," she said, wiping her mouth with the linen napkin.

"It will be nice to have you. I am sure Marsh will be overjoyed to see you.

It will be sad but very rewarding at the same time," she replied, finishing her salad.

The waitress brought us the bill, I paid for it, and we left the restaurant. We strolled past souvenir stores, cafes, candy stores, antique stores, and farmers' markets loaded with fresh fruits and vegetables. It was a beautiful afternoon, low humidity, and clear blue skies.

"Thanks so much for the nice lunch," Mum said, walking slowly along the wooden boards, holding on to my arm. She stopped and looked at me. "How do you know that sending others to the hereafter will help you?"

Her question surprised me but it made me think that she was considering going to the other side. We sat on a wooden bench and I told her the story of the injured seagull. "When I first came to the island, there was a bad storm, and a gull was hurt and squealing on the beach. I approached it with caution, tried to console it, but it fluttered away from me."

"What did you do then?" she asked, listening.

"I tried feeding it some food, fish scraps, and seed, and then it seemed to feel more comfortable with me. I was actually able to pet it. It also took food from my hand. This took a few days."

"Did it ever fly again?" she wondered.

"No, it struggled to flutter but could not fly. I put it in a box with a soft towel and carried it to the Realm

Incarnate. Mum, it was miraculous. I tossed the seagull into the air and it flew away, completely healed, and it glittered and shined like a dove. I suddenly felt more strength and energy. That is why I know this is for real."

"That is wonderful," she said, leaving the bench, heading down the boardwalk. Soon we approached the Ocean Walk Senior Home. She walked the stairs to the front door, waved, and then entered into the building. Though she did give me a direct answer, I was still skeptical about her coming tomorrow to the farewell for Marsh. I had to be optimistic and just believe. I left the senior home and headed down the boardwalk to the wooden bridge that led back home. I took my time across the wooden bridges, walkways, and trails past the dunes.

I enjoyed the walk past tropical plants, wild grasses, and palm trees. It was an enjoyable time for me. My mind was on Marsh and his departure. It was going to be tomorrow, my first venture, and I wanted everything to be perfect. Suddenly he appeared in front of me from behind a dune. I jumped and flung a startled look at him.

"I know what you are going to say, but I was anxious to see you."

I caught my breath and smacked his shoulder. "Why must you do that? You are going to give me a heart attack."

"You should expect it," he said. "When I want something, I want it now."

"Yes, I should be used to it," I laughed. "What is it?"

"Can you cut my hair again? That is all I need. Then I will be ready."

"No problem," I told him.

"How was your lunch with Mum?"

"I enjoyed her company very much. She is a remarkable woman."

"Is she going to move into the house?" he inquired.

"I don't know. We did not talk about it. She might be better off living at the senior home," I answered, trying to catch up to him.

"I just don't want you to be alone," Marsh answered, kicking his heels ahead of me. "She deserves to live with someone as nice as you. I know you would take good care of her."

"She might need special care?"

"No, she is capable of taking care of herself," he said, stopping, and then jumping ahead. "She even helps the other ladies at the home."

"Why are you so jumpy?"

"Just nervous," he answered. "I am going to a totally new place and I just want to make sure you will be okay back here. I know that by my departure you will get healthier, but at the same time I hate to leave you."

"I will be fine," I reassured him. "Just think of yourself."

He nodded his head, recoiled, and then walked ahead.

"Marsh, what would you have done if you would not have met me?"

He stopped in his tracks, wiped his sweating brow, and faced me. "I don't even want to think about it. I would have lived my miserable life by stealing, using others, getting free drugs, and even having sex to get what I want. I would travel to different countries and probably get into more trouble without finding true happiness. I have found what I want with you. You have changed my life, and I am ready for what lies ahead of me. I am scared but optimistic about my new life."

"I am happy to have helped you," I said, feeling reassured about his decision to go to the other side.

"Is Mum coming to my farewell?"

"Yes, she did tell me that she wanted to be there for you. She is coming on the ferryboat."

"Good, I want her to be there," he answered, running up the wooden stairs to the deck.

I set everything up for the hair cutting—clippers, a chair, and paper—and waited for Marsh. He returned wearing an old sheet and pounced on the chair. I gave him some papers to fill out while I cut his hair. I started from the back and came forward, cutting all of his hair and sideburns, and locks of hair fell to the ground.

"This might be our last day together," he commented, reading and signing the forms.

"Yes, you must have read my mind," I said, trimming his sides.

"You have helped me so much. I might have been a better person if I had met you a long time ago."

"Yes, you just needed some good guidance. You are on your way to a better place," I commented, brushing hair from his shoulders.

"Joah, I am so glad that I met you. I am feeling better already knowing that I don't look like my father. I hate this receding hairline," he said, pointing it out to me.

"You are all finished."

"Thanks so much," he commented, looking at himself in a mirror and handing me the signed papers.

He removed his sheet and tossed the excess hair over the balcony.

I gathered up the papers, checked to see if they were all correct, and placed them into a folder. Locking them into a secured cabinet, I went back onto the deck. I swept the excess hair onto the paper and tossed it into a garbage can. Marsh and I spent the rest of the day together, shared a dinner we both cooked, and sat on the deck and watched the sunset. It was a beautiful evening and vibrant colors stretched across the horizon and glistened over the water. We sat in awe and enjoyed the warm and breezy evening. Marsh went to bed early and I stayed on the deck relaxing in my rocking chair. Although I was exhausted from the long day, my mind was wide awake. I did not like the thought of being alone. Marsh was a very hyper guy, kept me active all of the time, but he was company. A sudden wind brushed across my shoulders and made me shiver. I wrapped a blanket around myself and fell asleep. Marsh woke me in the middle of the night and I went to bed. Rays of the sun peeked through the window, waking me, and I was filled with fear; Marsh was gone. Then I saw him and realized he was still at the house. I got out of bed, showered, and got ready for the ceremony.

I dressed in a blue polo shirt, khaki pants, and sandals. I shaved and brushed my hair; I wanted to look good for the presentation. I sat on the deck and waited for the ferryboat. Marsh joined me and sat across from me. We sat in silence, hardly breathing or looking at each other; it seemed as though a film of ice had covered us. The ice melted as Marsh spoke, "Well, this is it," he said as a boat whistle echoed in the distance.

"Yes, here comes the ferryboat," I commented.

Marsh rushed ahead of me to meet the guests and I trailed behind him. Father Leonard got off first and was dressed in a black outfit with a white collar; Colin was next, neatly groomed in a nice outfit; and Mum was next, dressed in a casual plaid dress with white shoes. They all greeted us.

"Hello, everyone," Father Leonard said, shaking hands and hugging everyone.

"This is Mum," Marsh said, introducing her to everyone.

"Nice to meet you," everyone said.

After all of the introductions, everyone got a chair and a drink and were escorted to the Realm Incarnate. Colin took his umbrella and a movie camera and took pictures as we talked and walked to the designated area. Everyone got situated on the beach and sat down, and Father Leonard gave the eulogy and last rites. It was a sad yet happy time as everyone waited in anticipation of Marsh's departure to the other side. When everything was complete, everyone left their chairs and walked across the dunes to the entrance. There were tears of sadness and happiness, hugs and kisses, and final words of kindness and farewell.

We left everyone and I took Marsh on a small boat to a small island. We strolled across the beach to the entrance of the Realm Incarnate. A sudden wind brushed across our shoulders as we entered into the dark tunnel. We experienced a sudden chill and then a warmth covered us like a blanket. It was an overwhelming feeling as sudden lights trailed everywhere, blinking and shining, and suddenly Marsh was gone. There was something new and refreshing, a new energy surrounding me, and I felt so strong and alive. The astounding feeling left me as I ventured back outside. I took the boat to the main island to be with the others.

Not a word was uttered as everyone gathered their things, trailed across the beach, and followed me back to the house. Mum held onto my hand, clung to me, and she was slower as we trailed behind everyone. Her entire body trembled.

"Joah, it was so beautiful. I know Marsh is in a better place. I feel it all through me; it is so real, and I can't help crying," she said, wiping her watery eyes.

"You have only a glimpse of how I feel. It is something unexplainable, something beyond belief—a feeling I have never experienced in all of my life."

Mum clung to my arm tightly as we came closer to the house, reminiscing about the past. "It saddens me that I couldn't help my husband. He lost his speech after his stroke and never got better. Even if I wanted to send him to the other side, he could not give an answer or make a decision. He had to suffer on this earth. Why?"

Her question and concern bewildered me and made me feel very helpless. Even with special powers, I could not help anyone who could not decide for themselves. There were hundreds of people out there with the same illnesses and sicknesses and I was not capable of relieving them from their pains. Tears welled up in my eyes as this reality consumed me.

Mum looked at my tear-filled eyes. "Why are you crying?"

"I guess I can't help everyone. I thought I could."

She grasped my arm and looked directly at me. "I thought I could too, but I couldn't bring my husband back and neither could you, so it was God's plan that he should suffer."

It just seemed so unfair, yet it was something I could not control or change, and something new to face in the future. I was lost for words as we neared the house and joined the others.

It was lunchtime and Father Leonard started the grill and began cooking hot dogs and hamburgers. I set the table with a seasonal cloth, napkins, silverware, a salad with Italian dressing, potato and macaroni salad, cups, and soda pop. There were cookies and brownies for dessert. Most of the delicacies were prepared by the guests, Marsh, and myself. It was our farewell to him.

Colin approached me and ducked in the shade. "Great farewell lunch. I am glad that I came."

I smiled at him and touched his shoulder. "It makes me feel good that you took time to come to the island."

"I know it is going to be difficult for you to be alone. I am planning on staying with you."

"Colin, don't do this for me; do it for you. I know you won't like being here at night, you don't like the sun, and you need someone to take care of your cat."

He nodded his head and thought for a moment. "You are right. I am just concerned about you."

"I will be fine," I said, munching on a hot dog and sipping soda.

"Though I was not fond of Marsh, some things he did say were inspiring," Colin said, nibbling potato salad.

Nodding, I urged him to continue.

"I will be with you to see others go to the other side; Marsh won't."

"That is so true, and I want you to be with me every step of the way." A solemn looked covered his face.

"And I want to be here for you," he said.

"That would be wonderful," I answered, finishing the lunch and carrying the plate to the trash.

Father Leonard approached me. "How are you handling everything?"

"I am doing okay. Thanks for asking," I answered, reassuring him.

"Is there anything I can do?"

"No, you have been a great help. The eulogy was beautiful, inspirational, and provocative. Thanks for being here."

"Joah, I was happy to be here. You are a very lucky guy to have such a special gift."

"I know, yet it is so rough to accept at times."

"I know you will miss Marsh. There will be others."

"He will always be special, my first," I answered, dodging his glance before I wept.

Everyone finished their lunches, talked and offered their farewells, and waited at the docks for the ferryboat. Mum offered to stay and help clean up the house. A loud whistle blew, the ferryboat docked, and then Father Leonard and Colin left the island. I waved to them as the boat disappeared across the horizon. Leaving the boat dock, I went back to the house. Mum sat on the deck fanning herself. I ran up the creaky stairs and took a seat next to her.

"You need a woman to keep this place clean," she commented, wiping sweat from her brow.

"I know I am not very neat," I said guiltily.

"There are two bags of garbage by the back door; I am too tired to take them to the junk pile."

"That is okay. I can take them later," I answered, looking away from her.

"What is it?" she inquired.

"Just something I saw on the beach."

She stood up and pointed. "It looks like a body."

"Oh my God, Marsh has returned," I said, jumping up and running down the stairs. I could not believe it. I was a failure. I sent him to the other side and he had returned. Once I got closer to the body, it resembled Marsh, but it was someone else. It was a thinner guy with dark skin and a bald head. His face was buried in the sand. I flipped him over and touched his wrist. He had a pulse. He was still alive. I tilted his head, opened his mouth, and gave him mouth-to-mouth resuscitation.

Mum raced toward me and watched.

The guy did not respond. There was no movement, and nothing was happening. I had not had a first-aid course in years; this was my first try, and I was not sure if I was doing it right. I was ready to run to my phone and call 911, but I thought by that time it might be too late. Suddenly there was coughing and choking, and water spurt from his mouth. My heart beat wildly as I waited for him to respond. His eyes opened. I helped him sit up and regain consciousness.

"How is he?" Mum inquired.

"I think he is okay. He is breathing."

"That is good. Who is he?" she wondered.

"I am Marcus," the stranger answered, coughing and spitting out sand.

"Nice to meet you; I am Joah and this is Mum," I said.

He nodded his head, rubbed his eyes, and looked around.

"Are you okay? Where are you from?" I asked.

"I am camping at a campground somewhere I must have had a seizure and fell into the ocean. The waves must have knocked me on shore."

"You are lucky to be alive."

"Yes, thanks so much," he said, standing and brushing the sand from his body.

Mum and I helped him to a chair and got him something to drink.

"Thank heavens you were here to rescue me," he said, sipping water from the glass I gave him.

"Yes, we were sitting on the deck and saw your body. How long were you in the ocean?"

"I must have had a seizure last night and fell into the ocean."

"Wow, it is almost three. That is amazing," Mum said, surprised.

"Would you like to stay here for a while and rest?"

"No, I should be getting back to camp. They will be worried about me."

"There should be a ferryboat arriving in about an hour or so, so you can come with me to the mainland. I live at the Ocean Walk Senior Home," she offered, handing him a towel.

That sounds like a good idea," he said, drying himself.

"Are you hungry?"

"No, just very nauseated and dizzy. I feel bad about intruding. Thanks for your hospitality," he said, sipping water.

"So you work at the camp?" I asked.

"No, I just go there on weekends to get away from my uncle and his son. I live with them."

"Do you have any other family?" Mum asked, handing him a bottled water.

"No, I have had a horrible family life. I feel they have caused my seizures. I am a very caring person with a soft heart for everyone, and they have used and abused me."

"That is too bad."

"I am sorry for laying this all on you. I should be going," he said, handing me the towel.

"If you ever need to get away, you are welcome here," I told him sincerely.

His big brown eyes lit up and a smile covered his face. "I appreciate the offer."

"The ferryboat should be coming shortly."

"Thanks. May I use your bathroom and shower to clean myself up?"

"Sure, follow me," I said, leading him up the stairs to the deck. I led him through the sliding door, took him upstairs, and handed him a fresh towel.

"I really appreciate this," he said, entering the bathroom and closing the door.

I ran back downstairs, looked for Mum, and sat next to her on the deck.

"What do you think of him?" she asked.

"I don't know. Do you think he is a runaway?" I wondered.

"No, he seems very sincere."

"Why did you offer to go with him on the ferryboat?" I inquired.

"He seems very harmless. Why did you offer to let him stay here?"

"I just thought it was the right thing to do."

"Same here," Mum said, agreeing.

We were both mesmerized and confused and did not know what to think of this guy. We waited for him to get ready, led him to the docks, and sat with him along the wooden walkway. There was a long silence and a very uncomfortable aura around us.

"I know you must think I am very strange, but you are just as strange as me living alone in the middle of nowhere in a house with hardly any furniture?"

His question caught me by surprise. He was feeling the same way we were.

"It is a long story. I came across this house during a storm and rebuilt the deck and remodeled the rooms, but then I got short on funds for furniture."

"It is a very nice place. We could pick up old furniture at flea markets and yard sales for cheaper prices. They are always having them on the island."

"Sounds like a good idea," I agreed, nodding.

"They also have picnics, dancing, hayrides, and campfires, which really relax me. You could come camping with me sometime."

"That would be real nice. Let me think about it," I answered.

Marcus turned toward Mum and looked at her. "Are you Joah's mother?

"No, my dear," she laughed. "I lost my husband last year and am still mourning him. Joah is just a good friend. I have other children."

A loud whistle echoed in the distance.

"It was so nice meeting you," I said, shaking Marcus's hand.

A ferryboat chugged through the water to the dock. The guides directed it into a docking area, parked it, and flung a walking ramp onto the dock.

I hugged Mum. Marcus helped her onto the ferryboat and they sat in a cool, shaded area. I stood on the dock until the boat faded into the horizon. A sudden breeze whistled through the trees. I shivered from the coolness and built a fire for warmth. This was not a pleasant time for me, being alone. Even though I had been by myself before, I always knew that Marsh was coming home. I was glad that he had gone to the other side of life. When Marcus appeared on the shore, I thought that something had gone wrong. Maybe I wish it would have happened because he would still be on the island. My vitality had returned and I felt very healthy, alert, and strong. It was not fair that I had to give up a friend to stay alive. I listened to some soft music and drifted asleep.

I was awakened by the soft rays of the sun and the whistle of a boat approaching the docks. I dressed in a blue tank top, shorts, and sandals. Running across the deck and down the stairs, I raced to the dock. Two people waved to me, Mum and Marcus, and they walked across the wooden ramp to greet me.

"This is a surprise," I said, hugging them and shaking their hands.

"We need your help," Mum said, pointing to all of the merchandise on the boat.

"What is all of this stuff?" I wondered.

"They are leftover things from my house. My children don't want any of it, so take what you want and the rest will go to Goodwill."

"That is so kind of you," I said, not knowing what to say.

"And I conned this young man into helping us," she laughed.

"So tell us what to do," Marcus said enthusiastically.

There were a lot of things on the boat that I needed for the house: a table and chairs, beds, dressers, a couch and a love seat, end tables, a coffee table and lamps, a bookcase, an entertainment center, and some sheets, bedspreads, and many other essential things. There was also a grill and deck furniture. Mum carried the lighter items and Marcus and I carried the heavier ones and placed them in the appropriate rooms. Mum motioned for Marcus to come toward me and then she went back to the ferryboat.

"Marcus, thanks so much for all of your help."

"No problem. I was glad to do it," he said, smiling.

"How did this all occur? I had no idea you were coming."

"It was Mum's idea. She made plans with me yesterday and we got together today and here we are," he said with a jittery tone.

"Are you going to stay for breakfast or lunch?"

Marcus shuffled his feet in the sand and stuttered. "I know you don't know me, but I need a place to stay. I can't stay with my uncle because his life is so unstable. I need a quiet and peaceful environment."

His request caught me by surprise. Although it would be nice to have someone stay, I knew nothing about seizures. I did not know where to begin.

"I don't have much money, just disability, but they are searching for a cure for my seizures, and I do take medication daily."

"I don't know anything about your illness, nor would I know what to do if something did happen to you."

"Don't worry about me. I can take care of myself. If I do have a seizure, all you have to do is tell me to relax and clam down."

"Let me think about this," I said, uncertain about what to do.

"Joah, I can help you and you can help me."

"What do you mean?" I wondered, surprised by his response.

"Mum told me that you were ill. I don't know what you have, but she said it can't be cured. You should not be living alone. Mum would like to move in and help you, but she would rather stay at the senior home."

"What else did Mum tell you?" I said, glaring at her from afar.

"Just that she helps with things at the senior home, goes to rosary, is in charge of bingo, sings in the choir, and is always baking cookies for the residents and her family."

"She told you more than she told me," I said, watching her dodge my glance.

"Can you give me a chance? How about if I stay just one night and if you can't handle me, then kick me out and send me back home."

I thought about his plan and nodded, "Okay."

He jumped into the air, waved to Mum, and went to unload some of his things.

I approached the boat and pointed a finger at Mum. "You had this all planned, didn't you?"

She dodged my glance and grunted, "Yes. So what?"

"Let me run my own life."

"Joah, I know what is best for you. Marcus can be a good friend and companion for you. I don't like you being alone. I also think that he will be your next victim to the other side."

"What makes you say that?"

"He deserves to go. He has been suffering all of his life. They can't find a cure for his seizures."

"It will be like the blind leading the blind."

"He is coming back," she said, motioning for me to be quiet.

"I am so glad that you are giving me a chance," he said, carrying his suitcases to the house. "I am taking the smaller bedroom facing the woods. I figured you would like the ocean-view room."

"That will be fine," I commented, waiting for him to leave.

"What do you know about him?"

"Just that he lives with his uncle who owns a bar, drinks, and has a mean temper and a messed-up life. He has a mom in Florida. I am sure he will give you names and numbers of others if you need to contact them. I have a good feeling about him. I am a good judge of people."

"Mum, I know nothing about seizures. It scares me."

She cleared her throat and grasped my arm. "Neither do I. Give it a chance. I need to go back to the mainland and get rid of my odds and ends. Workers from Goodwill will help me."

"Sounds good," I said, helping her onto the ferryboat and leading her to a seat in the shade.

"Let me know how everything goes. You know where I live," she laughed, sitting on a cushioned seat.

"I will," I told her, kissing her cheek. I left the boat, waved, and watched until it disappeared. Although I was not certain how everything would turn out, I was glad to have a new companion staying with me. I climbed the stairs to the wooden veranda and joined Marcus on a deck chair.

"I really like this place; it's very relaxing," he said, puffing on a cigarette.

"I didn't know you smoked," I commented, looking at him.

"I can put it out if it bothers you."

"No, that is okay. My ex-roommate used to smoke."

"What happened to him?" Marcus wondered.

"He needed to get his life together, so he went to another place."

He nodded, fidgeting in his chair and puffing on the cigarette. "And how did you meet Mum?"

"I met her through Marsh, my ex-roommate. He used to work with her at the nursing home. She was married for fifty years and lost her husband two weeks ago. He was an invalid for two years."

"I know. So what is wrong with you?" he asked, leaving his chair and leaning over the railing, crushing his cigarette on a deck board.

"I have an unknown disease, but I am getting better."

"Are you taking medication? I am taking all kinds of medication, but nothing works," he said, looking out at the ocean.

"No. It just has to work its way out of my system, like the common cold, but it just takes time," I explained, looking at him.

"I have had seizures since I was a child. They thought I was crazy until a teacher took time to analyze me and discovered my problem," he said, turning to face me.

"What a horrible way to live," I said, sympathizing with him.

"Yes, I need peace and stability. That is why I had to leave my uncle. His son antagonizes me. When Regis, my uncle, comes home from work, he is usually drunk and spills out all of his problems to me. I can't cope with it."

"I think you will find it refreshing here."

"I am already enjoying myself. Listen, can we build a fire tonight? That always relaxes me," he requested.

"That will be fine. I usually always have one anyway."

"Sounds great," he said, smiling and sitting back in his chair.

I went to the kitchen and got each of us a beverage. It was a hot afternoon. Handing one to Marcus, I asked, "How did you end up on the shore the other afternoon?"

He grasped the soda can, popped the lid, and sipped the liquid. "I don't know. I usually have my seizures in the morning. The last thing I remember was that I showered, went for a stroll on the beach, and awoke on your shore."

"That is an amazing story," I commented, sipping the cold soda.

"I am so glad you found me. I could have been swept up by a current, drowned, and died."

"I guess there was a reason for me finding you. If there were a way for you to escape all of your problems, would you take it?"

Marcus thought for a while and scratched his head. "Of course, I have been looking for a cure all of my life."

"Me too, me too," I nodded.

Marcus finished his drink and crushed his can. "The camp where I go is miles from here. I often wander. I saw you near a mound of earth one day, a dune, and you were crying. I did not want to bother you. Did someone very close to you die?" he inquired.

This situation caught me by surprise. I knew what I had to do, I had to tell him the truth even if it scared him away.

"There is something very important I have to tell you."

"What is it?" he jumped, wide-eyed.

"I have a gift and am able to send others to the other side of life without having to die."

"Where is this place?"

"The hereafter," I explained, finishing my can of soda.

"That is crazy!" he said, backing away from me.

"That is why I was crying at the mound. That is near the place where I sent Marsh."

"Why?" he trembled.

"He wanted to go."

"What made him want to go?"

"He was very unhappy with this life," I told him.

"This is way too much for me to handle right now," he explained, tossing his arms into the air.

"I completely understand," I said sincerely.

"Let me think about this," he answered, leaving the deck and going to his room.

I left him alone. I went to my room and began placing everything in order. I started with the bed and mattress and then got the desk, dresser, and nightstand in place. I hung blinds on the windows. I put new pillowcases, sheets, and an ocean-decorated bedspread on top of the blankets. I went through my clean clothes and placed them neatly in the drawers. I made room for picture frames, mail, keys, and my wallet. It was finally beginning to take shape.

When the sun faded and brought nightfall to the land, I got some wood together and made a nice fire. It was a cool evening, a perfect night for a fire, and I hoped it would draw Marcus outside. I placed deck chairs around it. I got lost in the sizzling embers and its warmth and faded into a trance. I looked through the flames and saw Marcus across from me. He remained silent.

Marcus placed another log on the fire. His eyes were glued to the flames. "I can't take anymore drama.

Unusual circumstances cause my seizures. I am staying tonight and leaving in the morning."

"That will be fine," I answered, nodding.

He returned to his seat and sweat beaded on his forehead. The fire grew more intense and I moved away from it.

"There's just something about fires that is so peaceful and wonderful," Marcus said, rubbing his palms.

"Yes, there's nothing like it," I commented.

We sat in silence and enjoyed the sparkling fire. The flames were intense and ripped through the logs. It burnt for hours until the charred wood began to change to ashes. The moon peeked through the palm trees and glowed over the fire, creating an eerie scene, and then a light breeze whipped through it.

"I don't know what to do. I don't want to go back to living with my uncle and his nephew; it's too intense and there are always problems with his mother. Regis also has a daughter through another woman, and the drama just gets to me."

"How does he treat you?" I asked, opening a bag of marshmallows.

"Very well, like a son, and he has helped me a great deal."

"Sometimes you have to accept the good with the bad," I told him, placing marshmallows on a large-handled fork.

"Yes, but I often leave and spend days at camp to get away."

"And your seizures still persist?"

"Yes. Not as many, but they are still there," he told me.

"How often do you take medication?" I asked, handing a cooked marshmallow to him.

"Once around noon and then at midnight," he said, munching.

"And when do you have your seizures?" I asked, licking my marshmallow-covered fingers.

"Mostly in the morning when I first wake up," he answered, placing another log on the fire.

Leaning forward, I looked at him. "I have never dealt with anyone with seizures before in my life. I have heard of them yet have never encountered anyone having one," I told him honestly, yawning.

"It is not so bad. I thrash around, run or jump, and howl like a werewolf."

"You are not serious," I laughed.

"Yes, I am, and I guess I feel the same way about you. I have never met someone who can take others to the hereafter."

"Does that make us even?" I guffawed.

"I guess it does," he answered, stretching.

"I think it is time for bed," I said, rubbing my eyes and trying to stay awake.

"I might sleep out here by the fire," he insisted.

"That will be fine. I have a sleeping bag if you want it."

"Sounds good," he nodded.

"It is in the closet near the entryway," I said, pointing to the house.

He left the fire and ran up the wooden stairs to the deck. He returned in a few minutes with a blanket and the sleeping bag.

"I hope you will be warm enough," I yawned, approaching the deck.

"I will be fine. Good night."

"Good night," I waved.

Sudden words echoed in the darkness. "If I am not here in the morning, thanks."

Stunned and not certain what to say, I howled like a wolf, "Whoa, whoa, whoa!"

Marcus disappeared under the sleeping bag and muttered, "Take me to the other side, take me to the other side."

Spurts of laughter shot out of both of us. The fire sparked wildly, and everything hissed and sputtered. As I climbed the stairs to the deck, I stopped and sat in a lounge chair.. I could not help thinking about Marcus. We were both burdened with problems and needed each other. It was the most joyous time I had had in a long time and I did not want to lose him. I did not want to think of him being gone when I awoke. Maybe it was because he scared me—I had never encountered anyone with seizures. Or maybe I did not want to see him return to his uncle. I was not sure if I could handle his problem. I was certain that he was thinking the same way and was wondering about me, my illness, and the hereafter. Or maybe I was just lonely. My eyes grew weary and I yawned. I went upstairs and lay in bed I took a deep breath, prayed, and closed my eyes and fell asleep.

Sudden rays of sun played over my face, awoke me, and made me jump. As I tossed on a pair of boxers and a tank top, I looked from my bedroom window, but I could not see Marcus. The ocean pounded on the shore, similar to the beating of my heart, and suddenly I could not breathe. I raced down the stairs to the deck, down another wooden stairway to the beach, and stopped near the place where Marcus was sleeping. He was gone. I could not believe it as I stared at the sleeping bag. I sat in a deck chair and wiped my dripping forehead as a sudden breeze cooled my body.

"About time you got up," a voice sounded behind me.

I jumped and turned around. "Marcus, where have you been?"

"I awoke early from the sun and the birds. I took a walk and found this blackberry patch," he said, handing me a basket of them.

"They are really juicy," I said, munching on a few of them.

Marcus sat down and leaned against the chair.

"Where did you get the basket?"

"I walked to the camping area where I often go. They had some in the gardeners shed."

"They are delicious. Don't you want some?" I asked.

"No, I had enough," he said, sticking out his purple tongue.

I laughed and continued munching on them.

"No seizures this morning. I awoke and felt really relaxed. The fire last night and the soothing ocean really helped me."

"That is great," I commented.

"It was so nice. I walked along the beach, kicked my feet though the ocean waves, and breathed in the fresh air. It was the perfect morning."

"Yes, this is a beautiful area. I like it here very much."

Marcus turned to face me, eye to eye, and smiled. "I sat on a rock and looked at the reflection of my lurid face, brown eyes, and disheveled dark hair in the water, and it made me realize I was not happy. Is your invitation still valid?

"Yes, it is. I was hoping you would change your mind," I smiled.

"I am going to shower, wash this sticky black hair of mine, and go see my uncle, talk to him, and pack up some things and bring them here."

"That will be fine," I agreed.

"How much do I need to stay here?"

Wondering how to answer him, I shrugged. "Just help me with repairs to the house and with food and chores, and we will go from there."

"It is a deal," he smiled, shaking my hand.

While Marcus was getting ready, I watered the petunias, snapdragons, geraniums, and ferns on the deck. The new water purifier was working well. I also watered the small vegetable garden close to the house. The green beans, lettuce, squash, cucumbers, and corn were doing well. They were sprouting and flowering. I pulled some weeds and adjusted the vines to help the beans grow and produce.

"Growing any marijuana here?" a gruff, feminine voice sounded.

I jumped and flipped around. "Who are you?"

"Josalynn," she said, staring at me. "Do you always roam around in your boxer shorts?" she asked, licking her lips.

"I was not expecting company," I answered, feeling naked and embarrassed.

She tossed her dark, curly hair aside and fumbled with her bikini strap. "I hate these things," she said, trying to adjust her boobs.

"Where are you from?" I asked, trying not to stare.

"I work as a housekeeper at a hotel not too far from here. I got done early and decided to stroll along the beach and saw you in those sexy boxers," she smiled.

"I am Joah. I live near here in a small beach house."

"I will come visit you sometime," she said, waving and turning. "By the way, did you know a guy named Marsh?"

Her sudden question stunned me. "Yes, I did know him."

"I have not seen him for a while. He left his job at the senior home. When was the last time you saw him?"

"It was a while ago."

"If you see him, tell him Josalynn says hello."

"Okay, I will," I answered, watching her leave. I did not receive very good vibes from her. Her sudden appearance stunned me and bothered me. There was just something about her that brought fear and doubt to my mind. I finished watering the plants and went back home.

When I returned to the house, Marcus was removing soot and charred wood from the fire pit. I paced the area. Breathing and looking in different directions, I could not relax. "Getting ready for another fire," I observed.

"Yes, I loved the fire last night."

"Me too," I answered, unenthused.

"Is there something wrong?" Marcus wondered.

"What makes you say that?"

"You seem jumpy, not like yourself," he said, observing my nervousness.

"You are very perceptive. This strange woman made advances on me."

"I would too if you were wearing those boxers. You can see everything," he laughed.

"Really?" I said, embarrassed.

"Who was she?"

"Her name is Josalynn. She works as a housekeeper in a hotel."

Marcus broke out laughing.

"What's so funny?"

"She is a well-known hooker; beware of her. She is also heavily into drugs."

"Wow, thanks for the warning. How do you know about her?"

"She often comes onto the guys at the camp, the owners and leaders, and is always looking for money. Keep away from her. She has very persuasive ways about her to lure you into her trap. Be careful," he warned, finishing up the pit cleaning.

"What are your plans for the rest of the day?"

Marcus stood up and pointed to the beach. "I am going back to the camp to pack up the rest of my things and go home. I saw one of the counselors this morning and told him what had happened. They were very concerned about my disappearance and felt bad about not watching me."

"Yes, that is their responsibility," I told him.

"Yes, I also packed a few things in this duffle bag," he said, pointing to it.

"What will your uncle say?"

"I will just tell him the truth and hopefully he will understand. I know he is concerned about me and wants me to be happy."

"Great! I will see you back here later tonight."

"Thanks for all of your help," he said, shaking my hand.

I watched him leave until he faded behind a dune. It was a beautiful morning with clear skies, a light breeze, and low humidity. I swept the wooden deck and arranged the new chairs from Mum around the railings. They were very attractive with cushioned seats. Then I went inside and arranged the chairs, love seat, couch, end tables, and coffee table around the room. A sudden knock at the door startled me. I wondered who it was. As I approached the glass door, I recognized the face immediately.

"Hey, Joah," a familiar voice rang out.

I opened the sliding door to let Colin into the house.

"You look petrified," he observed.

"No, I am fine," I answered, showing him into the living room.

"Where did you get all of the new pieces of furniture?" he wondered, looking around the area.

"Mum gave them to me. They are leftover items her family didn't need or want."

"You did a nice job of arranging everything," he said, strolling around the room.

"Thanks. I tried to make it look comfortable and livable," I told him, advancing to the kitchen. "Did you eat? How about coffee or breakfast?"

"No, I just ate. I thought I would come visit you since you are alone now."

"I may not be alone for long," I laughed.

"Is Mum moving in?"

"No, a guy named Marcus may be moving in this evening," I told him, pouring myself a cup of coffee.

"How did you meet him?" Colin inquired, leaning on the counter.

"He was unconscious on the beach. At first I thought it was Marsh."

"What a shock! What did you do?"

Choking on the coffee, I sputtered, "At first I did not know what to do and gave him mouth-to-mouth resuscitation."

"How did this happen? Who is he?"

"I revived him and talked to him. His name is Marcus. He was at a camp near here, developed a seizure, lost consciousness, and fell into the water. The waves washed him ashore."

"Wow, what a story! I might need some of that coffee," he said, taking a seat at the coffee bar.

I poured him a cup of java and placed it on the counter.

"Joah, you know nothing about seizures."

"Yes, I know. He only has them at certain times."

"This is a great responsibility. What if he has another seizure and is washed out into the ocean forever? It will be your fault," he said, sipping the hot coffee.

"I never thought about that," I said.

"Does he know about your gift?"

"Yes, at first he was very skeptical, but now he seems much more understanding and could possibly be another candidate to send to the other side."

"Does he have a family?" Colin wondered.

"Yes, he does. He lives with his uncle and cousin," I said, finishing my coffee.

"Why does he want to leave them?"

"It is just a bad situation. Drama causes him to have seizures. He needs to live in a calm and peaceful environment."

"This is definitely a good place for him," Colin agreed, finishing his coffee.

"Listen, I am going to change and go for a jog on the beach. It helps me relax and get my thoughts together," I told Colin.

"That sounds good. I need to do some work on the movie memorabilia and relax on the beach beneath my umbrella," he said, pointing to the umbrella.

"Sounds like a plan," I commented, going to my room and changing into running shorts. I rubbed some sunblock on my face and shoulders. I packed a few essential things into a small backpack and began my run. Usually my jogs on the ocean relaxed me, but this morning I felt stressed and uncomfortable. Negative thoughts of the woman I met at the garden filled my mind. There was just something evil about her. Just the way she talked, walked, and looked troubled me. Her aura was very creepy and sneaky like a slithering snake. I stopped and rested beneath a palm tree. Feeling dry and thirsty, I chugged a bottled water.

I recalled the first time I met Marsh on the beach. I snickered to myself as I thought of the embarrassment of being naked and vulnerable in front of him. It was a very uncomfortable first meeting. It still felt odd that he was gone.

I knew that Marcus was going to be a challenge for me. Colin was correct in stating that I knew nothing about seizures. I had heard of them and read about them, but I had never seen anyone have one. The fact that Marcus could have another seizure and drop into the ocean and be washed away was very devastating to me. It would be my fault. This was all etched into my mind. Each day I took a pen and wrote my thoughts down on paper.

I took a deep breath and continued my jog on the beach. Once I got closer to home, I noticed Colin sprawled out on a blanket beneath an umbrella. A sudden breeze tossed sand into his face, into his long hair, and he kept scratching and tossing his head. I stopped and took a seat next to him on the blanket.

"Did you enjoy your run?"

"Yes, it was very nice. I also did some writing," I told him, removing the bag from my shoulders.

"It is nice to see you using your creativity."

"Yes, I enjoy jotting my thoughts down on paper," I told him.

"Do you miss Marsh?"

"Yes, it has not been easy being alone. I do miss him. He was a lot of work. I spent days filling out forms to finalize his debts, and I put up with his indecisiveness and moods in order to get along with him. He often did a lot of strange things."

"Tell me about them," Colin insisted.

I leaned back on my arms and looked up at the sun. "For starters, he always liked to go swimming on dark and gloomy days. On sunny days he wanted to hide from the light."

"That is so odd," Colin laughed, hiding from the sun.

"Once he was swimming during a thunderstorm, returned, and was drenched from the ocean water and rain."

"He could have been struck by lightning," Colin said, concerned.

"I know. He would not listen to me. I often wanted him to come swimming with me on sunny days, but he insisted on sitting in a shaded corner."

"Tell me more," Colin insisted.

"One night after I had installed some fire alarms, he decided to cook a burger. I was in a deep sleep. He was cooking in the kitchen, set them off, and was uncertain what to do. I jumped up and flung open my bedroom door and he stood there clinging to the smoky burger and the alarm. 'Sorry,' he said."

Colin broke out into an uncontrollable laugh.

Smoke filled the air. I jumped up, opened the lid, and tossed some salt on the flames.

Colin waved his arms into the air to get rid of the smoke. "Joah, I am so sorry. I tossed some food on the grill and forgot about it. I wanted to surprise you with a meal."

"I am very surprised," I said, looking at the charred and salt-covered food.

"Is it all ruined?"

"Yes, unless you like well-done burgers and hot dogs," I said, turning off the grill.

A look of disappointment covered his face as he walked away.

"It could have happened to anyone."

"I am no better than Marsh," Colin said, getting his things together. "I could have started a fire."

"It was my fault for hogging the conversation and taking your mind off the grill."

Colin jumped and pointed a finger at my chest. "I do this all of the time. I am an accident ready to happen."

"You are just preoccupied with other things. Don't take it so seriously."

"I almost burnt down the church," he said, folding up his beach umbrella.

"How did you do that?"

"I was putting out the candles at Father Leonard's church, tossed a match into an ashtray, missed it, and some linens started on fire."

"That could have happened to anyone."

Colin turned and looked directly at me. "I have been seriously thinking about going to the other side. I have nothing here; I'm a failure. I live on welfare and S.S.I.. I survive by taking medications for anxiety, and they are making me forgetful. It really scares me."

"When did this occur?"

"It has been on my mind for a long time. I have tried several times to commit suicide, but I am a chicken and don't have the guts to kill myself. I am a hopeless case."

"Colin, just take it easy. I need you here."

"You need me to go to the other side so you can feel healthier. I don't like the ocean ,rays of the sun, can't stay in the heat, am afraid in the dark, and have so many fears and anxieties. I take medications for all of these things and they are not making me any better."

A sudden chill came over me, sweat beaded on my forehead, and I felt light-headed and faint. My entire body trembled. I sat in the shade, took several deep breaths, and struggled to regain consciousness. Clouds faded from my eyes, a coolness covered me, and I was back again.

"Joah, you don't deserve this," Colin observed, touching my forehead, placing a cold compress over my eyes.

"And you don't deserve what is happening to you," I answered.

"Yes, but the world needs you more than me. You have special abilities to help others. I have nothing to offer," he said, grabbing his black bag and umbrella.

"You also have a lot to offer," I said, trying to cheer him up, standing and removing the compress.

"I don't know what to say or how to answer you," he shrugged, walking along a trail behind the house to the dunes.

"You are always welcome here if you need to stay," I said, sympathizing with him, grasping his shoulder.

"I am sorry to lay all of this on you. It is just the way I am feeling today. I am going to the mainland to pick up some frames for some new photos," he said, waving and continuing onward.

Colin was heavily on my mind. There were so many problems troubling him, yet he feared taking his life, and he would never go to the other side unless I pushed him to go. He was not very courageous. I watched him until he faded into the distance.

I was still feeling dizzy and nauseated as I walked back to the house. I sat in a chair with the compress over my head and eyes hoping this horrible feeling would fade away.

A whistle sounded in the distance as the ferryboat approached the dock. I stood up and stumbled to it. Once it docked, Marcus appeared with suitcases and stepped across the wooden planks to the pier.

"Joah, what is wrong? You don't look too good," Marcus observed.

"Just a bit dizzy," I answered, helping him with his luggage and grocery bags.

"I can handle this by myself. Maybe you should sit and relax."

"No, I am okay," I said, feeling stronger and back to normal.

"Thanks," he said, unloading everything onto the pier.

"Is your uncle okay with everything?"

"As well as can be expected," Marcus answered, handing things to me.

I took a deep breath and leaned on the railing.

"Are you sure you are okay?" he asked with concern.

"It just comes and goes," I said, struggling to stand.

The ferryboat left the dock after everything was unloaded and floated away The chugging of the motor pounded in my head and the smoke made me cough and choke.

"Joah, you are worrying me."

"The only way I will get better is if others go to the other side. There is no cure for me," I told him, struggling to breathe.

"Why didn't you tell me this before?" Marcus wondered.

"I wanted to, believe me I did, but I have not felt this sick in months."

"So having Marsh go to the other side has helped you. Is this the only cure?"

"Yes, that is the only medication that will help me."

"We are both suffering, me with seizures and you with a disease without a cure. Just doesn't seem fair, does it?"

"No, it isn't fair," I answered, finally feeling stronger with a clear mind and head.

"My uncle thinks I will come running back like a dog with my tail between my legs," Marcus said, grabbing some of his things.

"What do you think?" I wondered, grabbing a few bags.

"I will never go back unless you die. I love the ocean and the warm fires on the shore," he answered, creaking over the wooden boards.

"That will never happen," I assured him, following.

"I hope not. I feel so much better already," he said, walking up the wooden stairs to the deck.

"I am sure you will be very happy here," I said, opening the sliding door and waiting for him to enter.

"I know I will," he said, climbing the stairs to the bedrooms.

I dropped his things into a corner as he looked around the room. He placed his luggage next to the bed and smiled. "This is such a nice room. I have been thinking about nothing except for living here and being free."

"Let's get the rest of your things. You can unpack and we can have a nice fire tonight."

"That sounds like a great idea," he smiled, racing me to the pier.

Marcus was a fast runner, but I beat him to the dock.

"Hey, who burnt all of the hamburgers and hot dogs? I noticed them charred in the grill," he said, grabbing a few more suitcases.

"Oh," I laughed, recalling the incident. "A good friend of mine, Colin, was just here and burnt them."

"Who is he and how did you meet him?"

"We have been friends for many years. He did a lot of the movie-star photos and pictures scattered around the rooms."

"He is very talented," Marcus said, leading the way to the house.

"Yes, he is very artistic. He comes here occasionally during the day and hides beneath an umbrella. He hates the sun; he is very light-skinned," I told him, following.

"I have olive skin, but I still have to protect myself from the sun's rays. I have gotten burnt before," Marcus said, leading the way to his room.

"Yep, you've got to use sunblock," I said, scattering bags around the room.

"I also brought some food, cereals, and milk. We can share them," he said, pointing to a blue bag.

"Good. We can always use extra food," I laughed, rubbing my stomach.

"I think I am going to like it here," he smiled, sitting on the bed.

"Yes, I hope you will be happy here," I said, grabbing the blue bag. "I will take this downstairs to the kitchen."

"I will come down shortly," he said, looking around the room.

"Good. I will start a fire outside. I know that will relax you."

"Thanks," he smiled, unpacking some of his things.

I carried the bag downstairs, unpacked it, and placed the groceries on the counter and in the refrigerator. I wondered if I was making a good decision. We were not strangers and I knew a little about him, but could Marcus be trusted and would we get along? These were questions on my mind. It is not easy living with someone new. It was a chance I had to take without fear.

I began gathering wood for a fire. There was rotted wood and branches scattered around the property, plenty for kindling, and I made a teepee of it. I placed old paper between the twigs and the fire began to flame.

Marcus came down a few minutes later dressed in a T-shirt and boxers and sat next to the fire rubbing his hands. "Nice fire," he observed.

"Thanks," I answered, tossing another log on it.

"Joah, do you ever get lonely out here by yourself?"

It was a question I had thought about over and over again. It was something new that troubled me and I had to face. It was part of my job to let others go to the other side and not miss them. Not prepared to answer, I said, "Marsh had brought that up with me."

"How did you answer him?" Marcus probed.

Though I was not ready to respond, I knew Marcus needed an answer. "I have always had plenty of friends and family. This is an entirely new thing for me."

"Have you had many girlfriends?"

"Yes, but most of the relationships have been stressful and disastrous."

Marcus lit a cigarette and winked, "Tell me."

"I will give you one experience," I said, shifting the logs on the fire.

Marcus nodded for me to continue.

"The last date I had was set up by a friend. I went to her house and a guy answered."

"Who was it?" he guffawed, choking.

"Her ex-husband. They lived together as roommates. Neither of them wanted to give up the house," I explained.

"How strange," he said as he puffed on his cigarette.

"We had a date to go out to dinner. I drove to the restaurant, stepped out of the car to open her door, and she was not there."

"Where did she go?" Marcus wondered.

"It was a snowy day and she slid on slush and ice and went under the car. I heard moans and cries, helped her up, and took her home. She was a total mess after the fall."

"That is hysterical," he laughed, lighting another cigarette. "Let me tell you about one of my experiences."

"Go for it," I said, edging him to begin.

"I dated a girl who was always late."

"What was her problem?" I wondered.

"She used to take long routes to avoid bridges. There were certain bridges that frightened her."

"How did you find out about her phobia?" I inquired, intrigued.

"We were crossing a bridge and she completely froze She hardly moved or breathed."

"That beats my story," I laughed.

"Sometimes I think it is better to live alone," he said, puffing.

I thought about his response. "I like my freedom yet don't like being alone. We had worked together for months, became good friends, and I was devastated when I had to let him go."

"He was gay, wasn't he?"

His reply caught me by surprise. "How did you know?"

He remained silent for a while and answered, "Josalynn told me."

I froze and trembled. "When did you see her?"

"I bumped into her at the mainland. I think I told you I knew her."

"Yes, you did," I replied, looking away from him.

"Was there anything between you and Marsh?"

"No, I am straight. He told me he was attracted to me, but I let him know that nothing would ever happen between us. My main purpose is to help others reach the other side, nothing more."

"So you are not interested in finding a mate?" Marcus inquired.

"No, not currently, especially since I am ill. I would not want to burden anyone with my sickness."

"And what if you get better?" Marcus asked, glaring into the fire.

"I will cross that bridge when I come to it," I laughed.

"That is a good way of looking at things," he said, catching the joke.

The warmth of the fire was very relaxing and refreshing. My eyes were glued to the blue flames.

"I have something to tell you," Marcus confessed.

"What is it?" I shuddered, chilled.

"I talked to Josalynn about your gift."

My mouth fell open in shock. "How could you do that?"

"It was on my mind and she dug it out of me. I am weak," he stuttered.

"I don't trust her. There is something evil and conniving about her," I said, jumping up and pacing.

"I am really sorry."

"Did she say anything about me?"

Not certain whether to tell me or not, Marcus dodged my glance and muttered, "She thinks you killed Marsh."

"And do you believe her? Why would I do that?"

"That is why I am confronting you with everything. I don't believe her."

"What would be my incentive to kill him?" I said, anxious to here his reply.

"Maybe to take his inheritance and insurance," he answered.

"He did not have anything!" I explained honestly.

"She thinks you used him to fix up your house so you would not have to pay a contractor."

"I taught him to build the house. He knew nothing. Where is she getting this information?"

"I don't have much money, so if you intend to do the same thing, I might as well leave now," Marcus said, glancing at me with his big brown eyes.

"My main concern is to get better by sending others to the other side of life. That is my goal," I explained, sitting and calming down.

"Thanks for being honest with me. Josalynn has a horrible reputation and she is not to be trusted. I trust you, I have from the start, and that is why I am here," he answered sincerely.

"That means a lot to me," I told him, relieved.

The fire fizzled out, our conversation grew sparse, and we parted. I went to my bedroom and Marcus remained by the fire. I sat in bed and could not sleep. I heard footsteps and the squeak of the bedroom door as Marcus went to bed. I wondered if he would have a seizure. I was not sure what to do if it occurred or how to go about helping him. I tossed and turned in bed and fell asleep. I was awakened by a squeaky bathroom door, water running in the bathroom, and the sputtering bathroom fan. Suddenly heavy footsteps and running echoed outside my door along with a howling sound. I jumped out of bed and saw Marcus pacing. "What are you doing?" I asked him.

He stopped and turned, looked at me, and clutched the handle of a closet door. He was breathless and sweat beaded on his forehead. He opened the closet door and stared. "Are you okay?" I inquired.

His eyes were glazed. "I am fine. What am I doing here?"

"I think you just had a seizure," I told him.

"It must be the new environment. Sorry," he said, returning to bed.

This sudden outburst awoke me and I could not sleep. I went downstairs and made myself a cup of coffee. It was not so bad, I thought to myself; I could handle his seizures. I was just afraid of him hurting himself. A whistle sounded outside and disturbed my thinking. Glancing from the kitchen window, I saw the ferryboat docking at the pier. I quickly dressed in a pair of shorts and a tank top and went to see who was arriving. I noticed the woman at once, Mum, and she was dressed in a stunning sundress and hat. "Hello," I waved to her.

She hobbled across the boat, held onto the handrails, and stepped onto the pier. "You never come to see me, so I decided to come and visit you."

"I have been busy with Marcus," I answered, grasping her hand and helping her across the pier.

"I am so glad he decided to stay," she said, glancing at me with her hazel eyes.

"He had a seizure this morning," I told her.

"Is he okay?" she inquired, concerned.

"Yes, it was not so bad; it was actually sort of funny," I said.

"It must be horrible to live like that each and every day without a cure," she answered, climbing the stairs to the deck.

"Yes, but I guess you learn to live with it just like my sickness," I said, following behind her and watching her.

Mum sat in a deck chair and fanned herself.

"Would you like a drink?"

"Yes, that and an ashtray," she said, removing a pack of cigarettes from her skirt.

"I did not know you smoked," I said, surprised.

"Yes, my one and only bad habit," she snickered.

"Is iced tea okay?"

"Anything," she said, removing her sun hat.

I found an ashtray and poured her a glass of iced tea. Handing the items to her, I took a seat next to her. "And how have you been?"

"Not too good. I awoke yesterday morning and felt fine. Suddenly I got very weak and light-headed, vomited with dry heaves, and clung to walls for support. I am not sure what it is."

"That is horrible," I said, touching her shoulder.

"It happens over and over again. I went to the hospital once and they could not come up with any solutions," she said, fanning herself and taking a drink.

"How do you feel now?"

"Okay, I guess. That is why I was thinking about going to the other side—I am already sick. I mean, should I wait to suffer and actually die or go with my own free will?"

"That is your decision."

She lit a cigarette and nodded. "My family will do okay without me. I think they are the ones causing my anxiety and high blood pressure. I don't have my husband anymore to calm me down. My daughter is always having money problems, my son is always fighting with his wife, and the grandkids seem out of control. I need to be with my spouse."

"Will they be okay with your decision?"

"Yes, I want to do it before I lose my sanity and can't make decisions on my own," she said, puffing on her cigarette.

"I think that is a good idea," I agreed.

"How do you like the furniture?"

"It is great and fits the rooms very nicely. You have to see how I have arranged everything inside the house."

"Maybe later," she answered, sipping her drink and smoking.

I thought about what Josalynn had proclaimed about me and confronted Mum about it. "You know you did not have to give me anything."

"I know. I wanted you to have the furniture," she said, crushing her cigarette into the ashtray.

"Do you trust my gift and believe in me?"

"Yes, I was with you when you sent Marsh to the other side."

"You know I am not doing this for my own personal gain?"

"Yes, why would I think that way?" Mum wondered.

I leaned forward and looked at her. "A woman named Josalynn has said some horrible things about me. She scares me."

"Who is she?" Mum inquired, lighting another cigarette.

"She is a hooker and roams the island."

"Why would anyone believe her? Look at her reputation."

"She is very conniving and believable."

"Others are judged by their actions and not their words," she quoted, sipping her iced tea.

"I never thought about it in that way."

"I would not worry about it," she reassured me, finishing her cigarette and crushing it into the ashtray. "I want to see how your new place looks."

"I will be honored to show you," I told her, standing and offering her my arm.

She stood up and hooked her arm into mine.

"It looks so nice," she said, looking around the rooms. "You have done a fantastic job of putting it all into place. I made a wise decision by giving it all to you."

"I am glad you approve," I laughed, sitting on a kitchen stoop.

Footsteps and creaking stairs were heard above us, and Marcus appeared at the stairwell. "Good morning," he said, grabbing a fresh cup of coffee, yawning.

"Hello," we both commented

"You look very nice," Marcus commented, joining us at the breakfast bar.

"Thanks. I am so glad you decided to stay with Joah."

"Yes, I like it here very much. I like the sounds of the ocean, the campfires, and the peaceful environment," he said, pouring cream and sugar into his cup and sitting at the coffee bar.

"How are you feeling this morning?" I asked.

"Uh oh, did I have a seizure?" he wondered.

"Yes, this morning," I told him.

"I faintly remember it. Did I scare you?"

"No, not really, just the howling," I laughed.

Marcus laughed and almost choked on his coffee. "The howling started when I had a seizure on an airplane. I awoke to the sounds of the air against the wings of the plane and began the unusual sound."

"Do you have any inclination of a seizure starting?" Mum inquired.

"No, my heart just starts beating very rapidly. Sometimes it is caused by thinking about something, a dream, or just the rage of the day. There is no determination of when it will occur."

"That is horrible. Have you had much therapy?"

"I have been in and out of hospitals and given tests and all kinds of medication, but nothing has come close to a cure."

Mum lowered her head in silence. "I am old and frail; you are young and should not have to suffer like this just to live a normal life."

"Mum, nothing is normal about my life," he said, sipping his coffee.

"It might do you good to relax here and find normality."

"It will never happen. I have to depend on drugs each and every day to control my seizures. They make me weak and tired and interfere with my sex life. My family is all screwed up and has caused a lot of my problems. They don't care about me and only think about themselves."

His words caught us by surprise.

"I hate to burden you both with all of this. I just want you both to know what is going on with me. I am going to get something to eat, take my medication, and shower," he said, finishing his coffee, leaving, and running upstairs.

"Just let him go," Mum said, stopping me.

"I should do something. He seems so upset," I said, jumping from my seat.

"He needs to think and analyze things. Just be there to listen and be his friend. That is what he needs more than anything else right now."

I calmed down and recoiled.

"Joah, why don't we go for a walk along the beach?" Mum suggested, lighting another cigarette.

"Yes, that sounds like a good idea. It is a beautiful morning," I agreed, leading the way from the house to the shore.

Mum followed closely behind me. She took a puff and exhaled. "There is a reason why I came here today, and after hearing Marcus's story, I have made up my mind."

"Tell me about it," I insisted, guessing, knowing.

"I have made up my mind and want to go to the other side. There is no reason for me being here. I want to be with my husband."

"What does your family think?"

"They are okay with it but skeptical," she answered, crushing her cigarette into the sand.

Sudden waves crashed on the shore and startled me.

"I would like Colin, Father Leonard, and Marcus to be there along with my family."

"That can be arranged," I told her, wondering, thinking. This was not an easy task for me, letting go and watching friends disappear from my life. This was my job on this earth. Sometimes I felt like Judas having to betray Christ; it was his task to perform, and I don't believe he wanted to do it. I felt the same way now. I know that sending Mum to the other side would help her and me, but it was difficult for me to lose a good friend.

"I appreciate it very much," she said, twisting her sun hat.

"When are you planning on going to the hereafter?"

She lit a cigarette and scratched her head. "I will let you know. I have to discuss everything with my family."

"Have you redeemed yourself and are you free of all debts?"

"I think I am. I will work with my family to make sure I am ready."

"I understand," I said, turning and heading back home.

"You have no idea how much I miss my husband," she wept.

"I have never had a spouse, but I can imagine how attached you can be to someone," I sympathized with her, wading through the water.

"Yes, fifty-plus years is a long time. I am fortunate and grateful for my time with him, but it is still not enough time," she said, holding her sun hat from blowing away.

"Mum, it saddens me to lose close friends like you. You have been with your husband for years and I have only known you for a month. It is so difficult losing loved ones. That is true love," I said, walking toward the pier.

"It should have been me, not him; he had to suffer so much," she said, strolling beside me.

"Yes, we often wonder why things have to be the way they are, and sometimes life does not seem fair."

"Thanks for being so sincere and understanding," she said, taking a seat on the dock.

We sat together and waited for the ferryboat. The whistle echoed in the distance, and the engine chugged and sputtered and sent fumes into the air. The ferryboat suddenly stopped and docked at the pier. I helped Mum onto the boat, got her situated, and kissed her good-bye. I left the boat and waved until it faded across the bay.

"I hope I did not send her away," a familiar voice echoed behind me. I turned and looked at Marcus eating a bowl of cereal. "It has nothing to do with you. She had something to discuss with me."

"Oh, hmm," he muttered, munching.

It was not something I was ready to face or talk about, yet I could not hold my thoughts or feelings inside of me.

"You might understand if you have ever been in love or in a relationship," I told him.

Marcus thought for a moment and nodded. "I thought I was in love, but it did not work out."

"Mum was married for over fifty years, longer than you and I have been alive, and she mourns and yearns for her late husband every day. The pain must be unbearable," I explained, walking to the house.

"Yes, there are all kinds of physical and emotional pain; I don't understand why we have to suffer so much," he said, finishing his cereal.

Turning and glancing into his eyes, I said, "Mum wants to go to the other side."

His eyes grew watery as he muttered, "This is quite a shock."

"I knew it would happen someday, but not so soon. She has done so much for me. I have grown so close to her," I said, sitting in a chair on the deck. I sensed Marcus had something on his mind by the look on his face, yet he was not ready to share it with me.

"I know what you mean. When is she planning this farewell?" he inquired, hiding his thoughts from me.

"She is undecided, but she wants you to be there," I said, shrugging.

"I want to be there. I really admire her."

"Marcus, she has given me so many beautiful things that I will cherish forever. It makes me sad."

I sniffed.

"She gave you things to make you happy, not sad," he told me.

His words made sense and made me think. "You are right. I need to focus more on her new life," I said, standing up and walking to the kitchen.

"That is the best thing to do," he agreed, following beside me with his cereal bowl and spoon.

"Thanks for your help," I said, grabbing a note pad and pen.

"Where are you going?" he asked.

"I am going to jog on the beach and do some writing," I told him.

"It must be great to be able to express your thoughts in writing. I will pick some vegetables from the garden for dinner. Have a good run," he said, running upstairs.

It was a sunny and warm afternoon, a perfect day for a jog. There was a nice breeze and not much humidity. I needed to take more time for myself to exercise and write. I wanted to write something each and every day, even if I was not in the mood to be creative. Writing was like a drug for me because once I created something, I felt high with a new zest for life. I placed a blanket on the beach, breathed in the fresh sea air, and began writing. My concentration was interrupted by a familiar voice, "Aren't you going skinny dipping?" I flung my head around and saw Josalynn behind me. "You startled me!" I exclaimed.

She sat next to me and tossed her hair in the breeze. "I just thought you liked showing off your body like me."

"I will never be like you."

"We have more in common than you think," she smiled, winking.

"Why are you stalking me?"

"I just want to know how you are getting away with everything," she snickered.

"You know nothing about me," I answered, dodging her glance.

"I thought we could be congenial to each other, but I guess not," she said, moving away, glancing out to sea.

"What do you want from me?"

"Just some answers. You took money from Marsh, Mum, and also from Marcus. He's a fool for believing you, but I know better," she said, gawking at me.

"My main concern is to help others."

"Then how did you get sick?"

"That is none of your business," I snapped.

"Fooling around with other guys, I bet," she grinned.

"You know that is a lie."

"Do I?" she answered, standing up. "If you were a real man, you would be jumping my bones. I am a sexy and aggressive woman."

"You are not my type and I am not interested."

"Most men would jump at a chance to be with me."

"Of course, as long as they pay for it," I said, grabbing my blanket and brushing off the sand.

"I learned from my mother and have taught my daughters to never sleep with a man unless they get something for it. Nothing comes free," she huffed.

"And that's called prostitution," I told her.

"Call it whatever you like," she said, circling the beach.

"I have done nothing wrong and feel no guilt," I told her, grasping my things and heading for home.

"I am married and have a wonderful husband. I have a job and work hard as a housekeeper. What do you have?"

I thought for a moment for an answer and looked at her. "I have a clear conscience and faith, something you will never have if you keep living your same miserable life," I said, moving away from her.

"How can you have peace of mind when you are lying and deceiving others by making them believe you are a prophet or something when you are nothing but a fake, taking all of their wealth for your gain?" she said, kicking the sand

I continued walking without uttering a word. I don't know why I let this woman get to me. I was doing God's will and deep in my heart I knew I was doing the right thing. Wealth and prosperity meant nothing to me. I started out with nothing and trusted in God. I was ill and could have been angry and condemned Him for it, but I accepted His will for me.

"Keep telling those lies," she guffawed, circling behind a dune and running away

Just the presence of Josalynn made me tremble and shake. I wanted to kick or smack a tree. I jogged across the beach and kicked the waves so hard that water splashed all around me. It bothered me that I got nothing done with my writing. She had destroyed my peaceful time of creativity. I ran so fast that I didn't realize I was already home. I looked ahead of me and noticed an unfamiliar person on the deck. I took a deep breath and proceeded to the house. The man worried me as I walked up the wooden steps.

"You must be Joah," he said, smiling.

His warm smile relaxed me. "Who are you?" I inquired.

"I am Dan, Mum's son," he answered, introducing himself.

"Nice to meet you," I said.

"Same here," he said, shaking my hand and sitting.

I sat next to him and wondered why he was there.

"I hope you don't mind me waiting here. Your roommate said it would be okay," he said, looking directly at me with his hazel eyes.

"You have Mum's eyes," I told him.

"Yes, they change from brown to green," he said, stroking his goatee.

"So what brings you here?"

He lowered his head in sorrow. "You know why I am here."

"Yes, to finalize the plans for Mum's farewell."

He lifted his head and nodded. "You are exactly right. It seems like just the other day that I lost my dad, and now I'm losing my mom."

"Talk to me about it," I said, motioning for him to continue.

"One day I went to my parents' house for lunch. They were not home, yet their car was still in the garage. This was very odd."

I listened to his story with concern.

"I pushed on the front door. It was ajar. They always had the door locked. I shoved it open and noticed overturned furniture."

"Were they robbed?" I shuddered frantically.

"That was my first thought. I ran around the house looking for them. I searched everywhere hoping they were not dead. The house was empty. I knew at this time that something was definitely wrong. The phone rang. I was relieved it was my brother and he informed me that Dad had a massive stroke."

"That is quite a story," I said, trembling.

"I was hoping it would be a good story with a happy ending, but dad never talked or got better for two years."

"That is awful!" I said, sympathizing with him.

He dried his eyes and sniffed. "We decided to let him go by using the hospice program. That is why I want Mom to be with Dad. They had a wonderful marriage. She deserves to be happy."

"I feel the same way," I answered, reassuring him.

"She went to the hospital each and every day to visit him unless there was bad weather or she was ill. That is true love."

"I knew she was a remarkable woman, but your story makes me think even more highly of her."

"I just want to make sure you are aware of everything."

"I appreciate that. You can trust me. I have already sent one person to the other side. She would like Father Leonard to give the eulogy and has invited a few of my friends."

"Yes, she has informed me about everything. We have taken care of her final wishes and will. What are the charges for your services?"

I leaned forward and shrugged. "Absolutely nothing. She has given me more than enough," I said, drying my eyes.

"I can't thank you enough. She would like to have the wake here, and the food will be catered. Here is a list of relatives who will be attending the services," he said, handing it to me.

This list caught me by surprise, as did having the food and services at my place. I would have a lot of preparation in the next two weeks. I could not say no to his requests. "It sounds wonderful."

"I will look forward to it," he said, standing up and walking across the deck.

"Do you have a way back?" I wondered.

"No, I am going to walk to the mainland. It is such a nice afternoon," he answered, going down the wooden stairs.

"Very nice meeting you," I said, waving to him. I watched him until he faded in the distance. Everything was happening too quickly. Two weeks was not a lot of time to get everything prepared and organized for her final farewell party. My thoughts were interrupted by the squeaking of a sliding door. I turned to face Marcus.

"I picked some fresh vegetables for dinner. How was your jog? Did you write anything?"

"No, it was not very relaxing. I ran into Josalynn," I said, approaching him and taking a seat on a lounge chair.

"Oh, ouch!" he said, stepping onto the deck.

"She is not to be trusted."

Marcus was silent as he sat next to me.

"Did you meet Dan?" I asked.

"Yes, he seems like a nice guy. Did everything go okay?"

"As well as can be expected, I guess. Mum wants to have the services and the party here. I have so much to do," I said, leaving my seat and looking out to sea.

"We will get it all done," he said confidently.

"I know. I just want everything to be perfect for her."

"I understand," he answered, looking at me with his big brown eyes.

"So, how have you been doing?" I inquired, leaning against the railing, sensing something in his voice.

"I am going to the hospital one more time to see if they can help me," he spat out.

"When are you going?" I asked, not ready for his answer.

"Next week," he cringed.

"Oh, great, so now I have to do everything myself," I snapped.

"It will only be for a few days," he reassured me.

"That won't be so bad," I recoiled.

"I want to give it one more chance. I am sick and tired of taking medication and it would be wonderful to live a normal life."

"That would be so nice for you," I said, sitting and calming down.

He turned toward me and muttered, "If it does not work, I want to go to the other side."

His decision caught me by surprise. It was a lot to digest in one day. This coming and going of people was difficult for me to comprehend. This was not going to be an easy time for me.

"I hate to burden you with all of this at one time," he said seriously.

"It is a part of my job that I need to handle with strength. I am not ready for all of these changes."

"I just want you to know what is going on with me," he told me.

I turned to him and smiled. "I appreciate your honesty and sincerity."

"Chances are I will be fine and you will be stuck with me for an eternity," he reassured me, snickering.

"I like your optimism," I told him. "What day are you going for your tests?"

"Monday," he stuttered, sweating.

"You will do fine. It will be lonely here without you."

"Then you have to come and visit me, because I hate hospitals," he said, standing and pacing.

"I will definitely be there as much as I can," I reassured him.

"I appreciate that very much," he answered, approaching the house.

I thought of all of the things facing me: Mum's party, the eulogy, Marcus going to the hospital and maybe going to the other side, and how to manage my time to get everything done. I had to quit worrying about everything. I placed my hands over my face in thought.

"I am going to get things ready for dinner. Don't panic, because I will be fine when I come out of the hospital and can help you get ready for the farewell party," he said, leaving and walking through the sliding door to the kitchen.

I lifted my head and wondered how he knew what I was thinking, how he read my mind, and suddenly I knew everything would turn out okay.

Mum's Farewell
Chapter Four

IT WAS A BUSY COUPLE of days getting things prepared for Mum's final party. The palm trees, shrubs, and tropical plants had to be trimmed and cut. There were broken limbs, twigs, and dried leaves that had to be picked up and removed. There were dead trees that had to be cut and the logs needed to be placed into a pile for firewood. Marcus and I disposed of the debris into a deep hole and covered it with sand. We raked and smoothed the front of the grounds and put down pebbles and fresh mulch. We set up a few tables beneath the trees and placed plastic tablecloths over them. I hoped it would not rain and make a mess of everything. I took Marcus to the hospital, checked him in, and got him situated in his room.

Colin came over the same day and helped set up aromatic candles throughout the rooms. He also set up bouquets of plastic flowers and fixed up an area outside for gifts of fresh flowers from the family. Colin brought several old frames and put pictures in them, past and present, and scattered them inside and outside.

Father Leonard arrived the next day on a ferry taxi covered with boxes of food, supplies, decorations, and luggage for Colin to stay for a few days. We unloaded everything and placed the items inside and outside in the rooms, closets, and cupboards and did not stop until it was all organized. Father Leonard had things to do, so he did not stay long, but we worked on the eulogy for the final party. Colin and I took a break for lunch. I made sandwiches and coffee for both of us.

"How have you been feeling?" Colin inquired, munching on a ham sandwich.

"Not too bad. My energy, vitality, and strength seem to have increased. I feel much healthier," I said, pouring coffee for both of us.

"That is great," he answered, wiping his dripping forehead with a napkin.

"Colin, you really don't have to stay. I know you don't like the hot sun or the beach," I said, sitting across from him at a wooden table.

"Joah, you need help to get things ready since Marcus is in the hospital. I am happy to be able to help you."

"It will only be for a few days," I said, munching on potato salad.

"It does not matter how long. I will stay as long as you need me," he said, sipping his coffee.

"Thanks so much for coming," I said, nodding and smiling.

"How is Marcus doing?" Colin inquired.

I laughed as I thought of the way Marcus looked in the hospital "He looks like a spider in a web with all of these wires connected to his head to be monitored."

"Does he seem to be in pain?" he wondered.

"No, just tired and aggravated with the staff and not being able to sleep," I said, munching on the sandwich.

"What about his tests?" Colin inquired, placing his coffee on the table.

"He has to remain in the hospital until he has a seizure so they can determine what part of the brain is causing the problems."

"What a horrible way to live," Colin said, saddened.

"Yes, he has put up with this all of his life."

"It would be nice for him to live a normal life without having to depend on drugs to stop the seizures," he commented, ducking from the rays of the sun.

"Yes, and hopefully something miraculous will happen for him."

"I know Father Leonard has been praying for him and having special services for his rapid recovery," Colin said, finishing his sandwich.

"I should attend services more often. I used to go every Sunday."

"He would love to see you," Colin said, finishing his coffee.

"I have been so busy working on the house, planting a garden, and getting things planned for Marsh and Mum, and being sick has not helped," I told Colin.

"Have you heard from Josalynn?"

I choked on my coffee and nodded. "Yes, I ran into her on one of my jogs on the beach. She thinks I am a liar and a fake."

"How could she claim such a thing? You are doing this to help others, not yourself, and she is the one who is living in sin. Don't let her get to you," Colin said with confidence and optimism.

"Yes, I know, yet something about her just makes me angry even though I know I am doing the right thing. Everything that has been given to me has been a gift from the heart. I had nothing when I first came to this island," I said, tossing paper plates into the garbage.

"Yes, I remember how decrepit this house was, and look how nice it looks now. That is quite an accomplishment," Colin said, patting my shoulder.

"This has all been possible thanks to you, Father Leonard, Marsh, Marcus, Mum, and gifts from the church. I appreciate it so much," I said, wiping a tear from my cheek.

"Joah, what is it?"

"Sometimes when I look around here, I miss Marsh so much. He was the first one to help me get everything together when the place was in shambles, and he is not here to enjoy it," I answered sadly.

"It must be difficult to let go. Is it going to be difficult to let Mum go?"

I stood up, leaned on the railing, and looked out to sea. I thought about his question. "Not as difficult as letting Marcus go," I replied.

"Marcus is going to the other side?" he asked, wondering if he had heard right.

I turned to face Colin. "Yes, if Marcus does not have luck with his tests, he is planning on going to the other side."

"When did he tell you this?" Colin asked, hardly able to speak.

"Just before he left for the hospital. That is why he is going to see if they can help him."

"Oh, Joah! What a horrible situation!"

"Colin, I am so glad that I have you to share my thoughts with and listen to my problems."

"I will always be here for you," he said, grabbing his belongings.

"Thanks so much for all of your help."

"I wish I could stay longer, but I have to get going," he said, advancing toward the stairs. His blue eyes twinkled as he waved and proceeded to the mainland.

I watched him until I could no longer see him. There was a lot on my mind and I was not sure how I was going to handle everything. I needed to relax and calm down. I took my writing tablet and blanket and found a quiet spot on the beach. I jotted down some words on paper. Usually the beaches were empty, but I noticed a figure in the distance, which enlarged into a man. It was Marcus. I waved to him as he approached me.

"They released me early from the hospital," he informed me, sitting next to me on the blanket.

"How did you know where to find me?" I wondered.

"I figured that since you were not home you might have gone for a walk on the beach," he said, brushing sand from his hairy legs.

"You should have told me yesterday when I was there that you were leaving today. I would have been there to meet you."

"I just decided this morning what to do," he said, lowering his head and pushing his toes through the sand.

"Tell me about it," I said, urging him to continue.

"Well, I had a seizure, which is good. I talked to a psychologist and a brain specialist."

"And what did they tell you?" I asked, anxiously awaiting his reply.

Marcus hesitated and got his thoughts together. "They told me that it is a very risky operation. I would be incoherent for months, and I could have a stroke and never talk or walk again. I could be a vegetable, and there is no guarantee," he said sadly.

"What are you going to do?" I wondered, waiting for a response.

"I decided not to go with the operation. I don't like having seizures, but I don't want to live the rest of my life in a coma," he answered, struggling to hold back his tears.

I hugged him, anticipating his next words.

"I have decided to go to the other side of life to live a normal life. It has to be better than this life," he wept.

Though I thought I was prepared for his answer, I was not, and I cried with him. I was hoping that something positive would happen for him.

"I have a few things to do before I go, things to straighten out in my life, and then I will let you know when I am ready to go," he said, pulling away from me.

"That will be fine," I said, wiping my tears.

"I am so glad that you found me on the beach. Now I can live in peace and harmony."

"Yes, this will help both of us," I said, trying to cheer him up.

"Listen, we should get going and get everything ready for Mum's farewell party. That is the main reason I wanted to leave the hospital early," he said, brushing the sand from his body and strolling toward the house.

"I appreciate it very much. I really need your help," I answered, grabbing my things and following him. It was a sunny and breezy afternoon and we enjoyed the walk to the house.

Caterers arrived and were scurrying around to get all of the food, hot and cold, set into place. There were pans of hot water with sterno cups beneath them for the hot foods and bowls of ice set up for the cold foods. Aromas of fresh food filled the air.

Mum arrived early and was dressed in a ravishing white lace dress, a plaid scarf, and a beige hat to protect her face from the sun. Her hair was styled and colored, her face was radiant in subtle makeup, and she smelt of lilacs. White sandals with straps adorned her feet.

"You look beautiful," I said, looking at her.

"I want to look good for my farewell," she smiled, coupling her arm into mine.

"You have never looked better," I told her, escorting her to the house.

"Thanks so much for all of your hard work. Everything looks beautiful," she commented, twisting and turning like a princess.

"Yes, and the weather has cooperated with us," I commented.

She stopped near the cake and read the writing, "Mr. and Mrs. Slinsky to be united again." Tears welled up in her eyes. "I am so happy," she wept.

"Then why are you crying?" I inquired.

"They are tears of sadness and happiness. I am happy to be reunited with my husband, yet I am saddened by leaving my family and friends."

"I can understand that," I said, taking her to a chair decorated with cloth and flowers.

"I feel like a princess," she smiled, touching the soft cotton material and smelling the fragrant flowers.

"They are all from family and friends."

She sat in the chair and closed her eyes. "My husband was a silent and peaceful man. He hated dealing with stress and pressure. He kept me calm. I have always been hyper and a worrier," she said, opening her eyes and lighting a cigarette.

I handed her an ashtray and sat beside her.

"He hated my smoking and would wave his arms, fling me a dirty look, and leave the room. I would always have to keep the kitchen door open and blow out the smoke," she said, flicking ashes into the tray.

"I can understand that," I said, intrigued by her story.

"He was a fixer of things: cars, furniture, pots and pans, windows and doors, and electrical items. He would have been a great help repairing this house."

"I wish I could have met him," I told her, listening.

"How is Marcus?" she inquired, changing the subject.

I shook my head in disappointment. "Not good," I told her.

"Oh, I am so sorry," she answered, having hoped for a miracle or cure.

"If they gave him the operation, it could make him an invalid for life. He does not want to live the rest of his life in a coma."

"So, is he going to the other side?"

"Yes, but he has not given me his final decision or date."

She leaned forward and touched my shoulder. "It is for the best. I think you and I knew it was going to happen."

"Yes, but not so soon," I said, looking away from her.

"This is supposed to be a joyous time, so be optimistic for me. My family and friends should be coming soon."

"I will try," I promised, smiling.

A sudden whistle and the chugging of an engine echoed in the distance as the taxi boat approached the dock. I escorted Mum to the pier and recognized some of the guests, but many of them were strangers to me. I strolled away from her and joined Marcus, Colin, and Father Leonard. We partook of chicken wings, cheese fries, and punch. The others joined us and slowly took seats around her chair as they brought her bouquets of flowers and plants to be displayed and admired. Mum was overjoyed with tears running down her cheeks. Father Leonard gave a short sermon, let her friends give their farewells, and ended with a beautiful eulogy.

I left them and felt led to go to the Realm Incarnate. I stood in front of it and prayed. It seemed like only yesterday that I was there with Marsh. I wondered how he was doing and if he was happy. Sometimes I longed to just get a glimpse of him, a smile, a feeling of his spirit, but nothing occurred or happened.

I suddenly felt weak and tired. My head started spinning and my legs felt like rubber. I struggled to breathe. I grabbed my chest and felt like I was going to pass out.

Father Leonard saw me and stopped the crowds of people. He raced toward me and grasped my shoulders, shook me, and lightly slapped my face. Suddenly I opened my eyes, breathed, and regained my sight. Father Leonard was vivid in front of me. "Thanks so much," I apologized.

"Are you okay?"

"I am fine. Let's get this over and done with," I told him.

Mum continued toward us with her family, relatives, and friends. Some of them remained at the house because they could not bear seeing her leave. She hugged and kissed everyone good-bye, and when she was ready, she joined me at the boat to take her to the Realm Incarnate. I took her arm and helped her to the front seat. Many of her relatives wanted to come, but this was something she had to do alone. She waved to everyone as we sped away. It was a short trip to the small island. I helped her from the boat and led her to the entrance. It was cool inside. The overwhelming feeling took over both of us. My dream came alive again and it was more beautiful and more peaceful than I could remember. It was similar to Christmas, a first love, the birth of a child, and nothing could compare to it. Many wonderful things had occurred in my life, but none came close to this feeling of awe. I stood near Mum as her spirit glowed in a heavenly light then faded away. She was gone.

I left the Realm Incarnate and sat on a dune and prayed. I felt so strong and alive. My entire body felt rejuvenated and reborn. It was nice to feel healthy once again. I left the island and drove the boat back to the island It was going to be difficult to face her loved ones without her. Once I docked the boat and stepped from it, all eyes were set on me. Many of her guests were crying in disbelief, some of them seemed skeptical, but most of them seemed overjoyed and happy for her. I joined all of them and escorted them back to the house. There was plenty of food to eat: chicken, potatoes, salads, rigatoni in a meat sauce, and lots of desserts. I was not hungry and talked with many of the guests. They hovered around her chair, touched it, and tried to rekindle her spirit. I tried to console them and make them feel at ease and peaceful. Mum did not want anyone to be unhappy or sad since she was at a better place with her husband. There were unbelievers with mixed feelings, but most of them accepted her departure The ferryboat taxi arrived a few hours later and everyone slowly boarded it and got ready to leave. I spoke to the guests as they ushered onto the dock. There were hugs and kisses shared among them and kind words of sympathy expressed, and then they drifted to their seats. The caterers packed up their things and also loaded their gear, tables and chairs, grills, heating pans, and other materials onto the boat. I did my best to direct everyone onto the boat. It was a sad yet happy time for everyone.

Father Leonard was one of the last to board the boat. He stood with me on the deck and shook my hand. "It was a very beautiful ceremony. You could feel the love and compassion of all of her guests."

"I totally agree. Your eulogy was beautiful. I really enjoyed the sermon and words of wisdom."

"You did a wonderful job of getting everything ready. It was very organized and well planned. The pictures really added to the significance of the day."

"It is thanks to all of my good friends, you, and Mum. I could not have done it without you."

There was a sudden clomping of feet, bags of things tossing in the wind, and a face hidden behind an umbrella as Colin almost ran into us. "I thought I was going to miss the boat," he breathed.

We laughed and helped him with his things.

"Joah, I know you did not eat, so I fixed you a plate of food and put it in the fridge," he said, folding his umbrella and ducking from the sun.

"Thanks. I am getting a bit hungry," I said, grabbing one of his bags.

"How are you feeling?" Father Leonard wondered.

"Okay," I shrugged. "I was feeling a bit woozy at the funeral."

"It is good to see you looking better," he said, moving ahead.

"Joah, I know you are going through a lot and I should stay with you, but my face is red from the sun. I need to put some lotion on it," he apologized, ducking beneath a shade.

"That is okay," I laughed, handing him one of his bags.

"I took some of the photos and frames with me, but just the ones that the family wants for keepsakes. I left a few for you next to the ones of Marsh."

"I appreciate your thoughtfulness," I said, hugging him.

"How are you handling everything?" Father Leonard inquired, taking a seat next to Colin.

"Not too well," I said honestly, "and each time I see something that Mum has given me, it makes me sad."

"If you need anything, let me know," he said sincerely, shaking my hand.

"I appreciate all that you have done for me."

The whistle blew, alarming everyone to board or leave the boat as it was ready to go. I waved to everyone and stepped from the boat to the pier. I watched it pull from the dock and sputter away across the horizon. It was all over and Mum was gone.

I walked toward the house and heard a gruff voice and snoring. Marcus was asleep on a deck chair. I went into the kitchen, looked for the plate of food, and heated it in the microwave. There was chicken, pork, and pasta with sauce along with some vegetables. I grabbed a glass of soda and the plate and took a seat on the deck.

Marcus squinted, opened one eye, and stretched. "The sun always puts me to sleep."

"That is okay. You deserve to sleep. It was a very demanding day," I told him, munching on some vegetables.

"The food was really good," he said, struggling to wake up.

"Yes, very tasty and appetizing," I said, eating a piece of chicken.

"I hate depending on this medication; it makes me drowsy," he apologized, turning on some light music on the stereo.

"Dinner music," I laughed.

"Do you like this group? They have a lot of melodic songs," he said, waking up.

"I really like any kind of music."

"Did everyone enjoy the food and services?" Marcus inquired.

"Yes, I think it was a success," I said, sipping soda.

Marcus leaned forward and looked at me with his big brown eyes. "Father Leonard gave a wonderful sermon. What must I do to prepare for the other side?"

I finished my meal and thought about his question. I stood up and tossed the plate and can into the garbage. "Why don't we go for a stroll on the beach. Would you like to go?"

"Sounds like a good idea," he said, turning off the music and following me.

I kicked through the sand and looked out to sea. The tides were low, it was late afternoon, and the waves crashed on the shore and released a cool mist into the air.

Marcus placed sunglasses on his face and caught up to me. "Where are we going?"

"To a place I have not gone to for a long time."

"Where might that be?"

"A place I go for light and inspiration."

Marcus followed me with a look of puzzlement on his face.

"You must redeem yourself by forgiving yourself and others. We have all made mistakes, but if we ask for forgiveness from God, we can be redeemed."

"What if we hold grudges against others?"

"You have to let it go and forgive," I told him.

"Should we go to these people and tell them they are forgiven?" Marcus wondered, struggling through the mounds of sand.

"Only if you feel you have to and can't forgive them in your heart. If it is bothering you and holding you back, then it is something you should do."

Marcus was silent as he walked beside me.

"There it is," I said, pointing to a huge structure in the distance.

"It is a lighthouse," Marcus said, surprised.

We stepped through two large wooden doors to the lobby, which circled into a souvenir stand. It was decorated in beach paraphernalia and beachwear along with books, magazines, and newspapers. There were also replicas of the lighthouse, small and large, plastic and wood, with scenery and people around them. We were amazed by the stuffed animals, pillows, bedding, and assorted candies and foods. We browsed for a few minutes and purchased tickets to walk to the top before they closed the doors in two hours.

"Are we walking to the top?" Marcus inquired, breathing heavily.

"Yes, walking is very good for stress, thinking, and clearing your mind."

"I guess so," he said, following me to the first stairwell.

"This place has such great history. It has stood strong through floods, hurricanes, and erosion."

"Wonderful," he said, panting

They used to carry hot oil all the way up these stairs to keep the light lit, and now they have a prism light. The view from the top is amazing."

"I can hardly wait," he said, stopping and sitting on a stoop.

"Is this too strenuous for you?" I inquired.

"No, I need to tell you something."

"What is it?" I asked, sitting next to him.

Marcus caught his breath and looked away from me. "Josalynn is my ex-girlfriend."

"Oh no," I said, standing and leaning on the railing.

"She is the one who I need to forgive," he said, approaching me and not looking down.

"What did she do?" I wondered, turning to face him.

"She cheated on me with another man," he said, looking faint.

"Are you okay?"

"Yes, sometimes heights make me nervous."

"Should we go back down?" I suggested.

"No, I will be okay. I want to see the view from the top," he said, pointing to the stairs.

"Marcus, she cheated on you. She should be the one asking you for forgiveness."

"She has asked me but I have not forgiven her. It is something that I have to do," he said, leading the way up the stairwell.

"I have never been in your situation, but I imagine it is not an easy task."

"Not at all," he said, reaching the top and opening a large door leading to the deck.

I stood beside Marcus thinking the height would scare him, but instead a look of awe covered his face. He looked calm and relaxed. I leaned on the railing and looked out to sea. The crashing of the ocean waves echoed and seemed twice as loud. There were villages, seascapes, boats and cars, and people walking below. There was so much to see—an entire world going on around us. We circled the upper terrace and stood in amazement peering at each new scene. There were binoculars, so we placed coins into them to get a better view of the scenery.

"This is just a glimpse of what the Realm Incarnate feels like," I told Marcus.

"I am just overwhelmed," he said, looking below.

"This is where I finally decided to change my life."

"What do you mean?" he wondered.

"I felt numbed and wanted to end my life. I was tired of my worthless life as a writer. It was the same boring job day after day," I told him, kicking the railing.

"What made you change your ways?"

"I discovered the Realm Incarnate. I fought the responsibility. I thought of all of the sad people with horrible lives who lived in constant pain. I had the ability to help them. I needed to live and begin my exploration."

"I am so glad you did," he said, smiling.

The wind wisped through my long hair and made me shiver. It was a nice feeling, finally doing something good for myself and others, and I was glad I made the right decision. I was prepared to face the challenges ahead of me. We circled the top of the lighthouse a few more times and enjoyed the beautiful scenery. A sudden wind whirled around us and made us shiver. We left the platform through the large wooden door, ducked into the corridor, and looked around the area. It was warmer inside. There was a revolving prism with rainbow colors twirling in many revolutions. It glowed as sunlight peeked through the glass windows.

"This lighthouse has existed here for centuries. It has a lot of history," I told him, pointing to the newspaper articles in frames on the walls.

"Yes, it even has a story about a ghost that might still exist along the stairway, a woman who shrieks and howls at her husband for bringing her to this isolated hell."

"Yes, I did read a story about her loneliness and being away from her family and friends," I said. "A storm knocked her from the top of the lighthouse and she fell onto the boulders and died."

"It is like my life with my seizures; I want to fade from my living hell," Marcus said, starting down the stairs.

"I will be your light and lead you to safety," I laughed, following behind him.

It was getting late and we rushed down the stairs—it was much easier to go down than up—and started back to the house. It was a remarkable day, a memorable one for both of us, and we both felt refreshed and relaxed. It was about to end when I saw a police boat docked near the pier. We both looked at each other in amazement as we neared the house. Two burly looking policemen stood below the deck peering at us. We approached them and wondered what was wrong.

One of them with a bald head introduced himself. "I am Officer Jenkins and this is Officer O'Reilly. May we speak with you for a moment?"

"Yes, what can I do for you?" I asked, leading them up the stairs to the deck chairs.

"We need to ask you a few questions," said Officer Jenkins, sitting in a deck chair. Officer O'Reilly sat next to him. Marcus left and went into the house.

"What is this all about?" I asked.

"I know you have had different roommates here. A woman gave us some crazy information about you helping others to die. Is this true?"

"Something like that," I answered.

They were silent for a moment, whispering and exchanging notes, and then turned to me. "Are you Joah Sloan?"

"Yes, you have the right person."

There was another brief silence "There was a dead body found on the shore close to here. They are not sure who it is and we just wanted you to know," they told me, standing up.

"Who found the body?

"Josalynn Conner. Do you know her?"

"Yes, we have spoken," I told them.

"We are just checking with all of the tourists, guests, and residents in the area. Thanks for your time," they said, shaking my hand.

"Thanks for stopping by," I told them, escorting them to the shore. They left the premises. I climbed the stairs to the deck.

"What is going on?" Marcus asked, standing in the doorway.

I sat in a deck chair and motioned for him to sit down. I ran my fingers through my hair and rubbed my forehead.

Marcus took a seat next to me.

"There was a dead body found on the shore."

Marcus sat in amazement, motionless, with his mouth wide open.

"They are not sure if it is male or female, but it was found by Josalynn."

"That is crazy! It could be anyone."

"What if it was Marsh or Mum?" I stuttered, concerned and confused.

"Why would you think that?"

"Maybe I am not as gifted as I thought I was," I answered, wondering.

"You saw both of them leave. You have to believe in yourself."

"I do. Maybe I just wish they were back. I miss them."

"I do too. I really believe they are with their creator."

"Why can't I see them or hear from them, a message or something to tell me how they are?" I trembled, pointing out to sea.

"I would be more concerned about Josalynn. You never know what might be on her mind," Marcus said, warning me.

"Yes, you do know her better than I. I should be more concerned about you. You have to forgive her to get on with your life."

"Yes, I need to get prepared to go to the other side," he told me, standing up.

"Where are you going?"

"I need to go to the drugstore on the mainland to get more of my medication. I will be back for dinner."

"That will be fine," I nodded. "I am going to take a stroll on the beach and do some writing."

"Sounds like a good idea. It might be good for you to relax after this trying day," he said, leaving the deck and walking toward the mainland.

I changed into running shorts and placed some writing items into a backpack, secured it on my shoulders, and began my run. It was a warm and muggy evening, dark clouds covered the sky and a sudden raindrop fell on my face. I ducked for cover before it began to storm. There was a dune with an opening, so I turned the corner and hid beneath it. Thunder pounded in the sky and large raindrops fell to the ground. Lightning hissed and flickered in sporadic forms over the horizon. Storms frightened me. Something else alarmed me. I was not alone. I turned my head and saw a woman huddled in a corner with drenched hair and clothes.

"This is a surprise," she sputtered, ringing her wet hair.

I couldn't see her face for the darkness, but I recognized the voice as that of Josalynn. She was the last person I wanted to see or be with in a storm. I prayed for the rain to stop.

"Isn't this quaint, the two of us being together in the same place. Who would of thought?" she snickered.

I stood in the corridor looking out at the rain. "It looks like it is stopping."

A loud clap of thunder sounded and made the ground tremble.

"I think you should sit and relax," she said, shaking her wet head. She handed me a cloth to wipe my dripping head and face.

"Thanks," I said, wiping my brow.

"You have no idea how attracted I was to you at one time, do you?"

"I never knew you had an attraction to me," I confessed.

She stared at me and dried the back of my head. "I had seen you many times on the shore, writing and thinking, swimming naked, and so many times I wanted to approach you."

"Why didn't you?" I asked, pushing her away.

She flung an angry look at me. "Marsh was also attracted to you. I saw him one day gawking at you. I warned him to leave you alone. I told him that you were mine. We fought over you. He had more balls than I did and went after you. I let it go. I thought if you took him home with you, then you were gay."

"You know that is not true."

"You took him home with you; what does that tell you?" she huffed.

"I needed help to repair my house and he needed a friend."

"A lover," she interrupted.

"And I let him stay with me in order to straighten out his life and go to the other side. I did not know he was gay."

"Oh, come on, look at the way he talked and acted," she said, imitating him.

"I don't judge others for what they are, but for who they are inside," I told her.

A sudden wind brushed sand beneath the dune.

"You are not fooling me at all," she said, pointing at my chest.

I brushed sand from my face and eyes. "Just believe what you want," I said, looking outside.

"I believe what I see," she said, glaring at me.

"You are just jealous because you always get what you want and you can't have me."

"I don't want you," she snickered, walking in circles.

"So why are you making such a big stink about everything?"

"The only thing that stinks here is your body," she sniffed.

"How am I supposed to smell with wet clothes?" I asked angrily.

"You don't know what I am trying to say. Your lies and insincerity make you a fake," she said, pacing.

"And you are believable?" I questioned her.

"I am an open book. Nothing you say fits together."

"And cheating on Marcus fits together?" I asked.

Her face tightened and she gritted her teeth. "He deserved it. He was never around because he was always working, and his seizures drove me crazy. I would stay up all night wondering if he would awake and knock all of my valuables onto the ground. He broke so many things of mine."

"You knew that before you met him."

"I know. I thought it would work out, but it was not meant to be."

"That gave you no right to cheat on him."

She combed through her drenched hair with her fingers and twisted in anguish. "I don't want Marcus to go to the other side."

"Did he talk to you about it?"

"Yes, that is absurd. I told him not to trust you."

"You are preventing him from being safe and free. He deserves to have a better life without seizures. Why would you do this to him?"

"I don't want to let him go. I know there is nothing between us, but at least I still get to see him," she shrugged, leaning on the side of the dune.

"But you are not being fair to him."

"And you are by promising him something that will never happen?" she said, laughing.

"He needs to feel forgiven. He still has hurt and pain from you."

"I will never release him. I have a hold on him," she said smugly.

"And what good is it to prevent him from eternal happiness?"

"I don't have it and no one else should have it," she snapped.

"Oh, you make me so angry," I said, trying to control myself.

"I am perfectly fine," she said, removing her wet clothes.

"What are you doing?" I said, staring.

"I just want you to see what you are missing."

"You have nothing I want," I answered, looking away from her.

"I know you are very horny and have not had it for a while. Just indulge," she said, acting very seductive.

"Not until you tell me whose body you found sprawled on the beach."

"You really know how to ruin a good moment," she huffed, covering herself.

"Is it Marsh?"

"It could be," she answered, buttoning her blouse.

"I don't believe you. You are a liar."

"Then why did you ask me?" she inquired.

"I just want to know."

"It is a male," she said, pulling on her jogging pants.

"When did you find the body?"

"I tripped over it late last night. It must have washed up on shore. It was tangled in seaweed, moss, and chipped shells. I thought it was a mound of sand or something."

"It must have really frightened you," I said, concerned.

"Yes, it was quite a shock," she answered, brushing sand from her clothes.

"What were you doing on the beach so late at night?"

"Enjoying a sensuous time with a friend," she said, licking her lips.

"Do you ever get tired of deceiving others?"

"Do you?" she smiled.

I shook my head in disbelief.

"You think I am a cold-hearted bitch, don't you?"

"What do you expect me to think?"

"The rain stopped," she said, stepping outside.

Our conversation had gotten so intense that I did not realize the rain had stopped and the sun was shining brightly in the sky. My entire body shivered from the dampness and the conversation with Josalynn. I stepped into the sun and enjoyed the warmth.

"You must never tell Marcus about any of this."

"He has a right to know. Why should I deny him his rights?"

"Do what I say. This is just a warning. I can make things very difficult and intense for you. Don't fuck with me!" she said abruptly.

Her harsh words frightened me, yet I was determined not to let it show. "You can never harm me. I have too much pride and confidence in myself to let someone like you get to me."

She took a deep breath, released it, and spat out saliva. "Then I will have to do what I have to do," she said, grinding her spit into the ground.

Her words startled me because I had no idea what she had on her mind. I knew what she was capable of doing and did not want to know. Sweat beaded on my forehead. My eyes burned as I watched her walk away and fade behind a dune. I was not certain what I wanted to do since Josalynn had ruined my day. Her harsh words had put me in a bad mood. I had to force my way out of these negative feelings and write my thoughts down on paper. I strolled along the beach, found a place beneath some palm trees, and stayed until dusk. The ocean waves roared all around me and sent a cool mist into the air. There was a blazing fire on the shore when I returned home. I sat in a canvas chair next to Marcus.

"I was worried about you in that storm. Where were you?" Marcus asked, concerned.

"I ducked beneath a sand dune until the storm ceased and then did some writing," I said, enjoying the warmth of the fire.

"Did you eat dinner? There is a lot of food left over from the going-away party for Mum" he said, tossing some logs on the fire.

"I will get something to eat later," I said, rubbing my hands to get warm.

"I got my medication for another month. It will be enough until I go to the other side."

"That is good news. Have you talked to Josalynn about the hereafter?"

He stared into the fire and thought for a moment. "Yes, I did tell her about my venture to go to the other side. She does not want me to go. She refuses to grant me forgiveness."

"How could you get involved with someone like her?" I asked, wondering.

"She was kind and sensitive to my needs and was willing to take care of me. I thought our friendship would grow into love and happiness forever. I often angered her with my seizures and broke some of her valuable trinkets. I did not do it on purpose," he said, glancing at me with his sad eyes.

"I believe you. She knew all about you when you moved in with her."

"I never thought she could be so mean and evil. I was deceived by her," he said, wiping a tear from his eye.

"She can be very deceptive," I said, agreeing.

"She lured me to her in seductive ways. Everyone told me about her but I refused to believe them. I was living with rose-colored glasses over my eyes. There were times when she was out late at night and I thought she was working, but she was out making money by sleeping with other guys. I pretended she was my one and only. I was such a fool," he said, feeling very used and humiliated.

"We all make mistakes in our lives," I told him sincerely.

"Now I have a chance to be free of my seizures and this life and she is putting it all on hold," he said sadly.

"We just have to hope for the best. Don't give up," I told him.

"What will happen if I go to the Realm Incarnate without redemption?" he asked, wondering.

"I don't know if you will be accepted," I told him honestly.

"Has anyone been refused?" he asked, concerned.

I was not ready for this question and I did not want to put anyone in jeopardy, but at the same time, I did not want to deceive him. "Another friend of mine, but he is working on it."

"Who is it?" he asked anxiously.

"I can't tell you; I promised him I would keep it a secret."

"Josalynn thinks the dead body on the shore is Marsh. Is it?"

"I think it is the guy who used to own this house. He was never found," I told him with confidence.

"Tell me about him," he insisted.

"He lived here with his wife and she left him. He loved the ocean and did not want to leave. There was a horrible storm that destroyed the house. He did not have money to fix it and either killed himself or drowned. His insurance money covered the cost of the house. It was left abandoned."

"Where is his wife?"

It had been a long day and I was not ready for all of these questions. There was enough facing me right now. My patience was running low and this was taking a toll on me. "I don't know," I shrugged.

"Have they contacted her?"

"Yes, but they can't find her whereabouts," I said, fidgeting.

"What if she comes back and claims the house?"

"It is something I might have to face in the near future," I said, hoping it would never happen.

"Where would you go if you could not live here?"

"No more stupid questions!" I snapped, standing and pacing.

"What is wrong with you?" he jumped, shocked.

"It is just too much to handle," I confessed, shaking.

"Is there anything I can do?" he asked sincerely.

"Just get ready for the other side," I commanded.

Marcus approached me with concern. "Something else happened today, didn't it."

"No, it has just been a long day with Mum's farewell, the police, and many other things."

"Let me help if I can."

"I will let you know if I need your assistance," I told him, leaving and going into the house. I was at a point where I was so tired that my body ached. A restful sleep would definitely help me to get my thoughts together to face another day My health was returning, yet everything else was falling apart. I went to my room, wrote some thoughts on paper, and then drifted to sleep. Nothing resurfaced until I was awakened the next day by Marcus. I twisted and turned trying to awake.

"Officer Jenkins is here to see you. Do you want to talk to him?"

"Yes, just offer him some coffee and let me awake and get dressed," I told Marcus, stretching and getting out of bed. I put a blue shirt on and pulled on a pair of running shorts. I glanced into a mirror, tossed my hair into place, and tried to look presentable. Slipping into a pair of sandals, I rushed down the stairs, poured myself a cup of coffee, and joined the officer on the deck. "Hello," I said, shaking his hand.

"Sorry to disturb you so early. I thought this might be important."

"No problem," I answered, sitting across from him.

He fumbled through some papers and looked at me. "How long have you lived here?"

"It has been about six months," I answered.

"You have had several people living with you, correct?"

"Just two, Marsh and Marcus," I answered.

"You don't own this house, do you?"

"No, they gave me the rights to live here if I fixed up the premises."

"You have done a good job," he said, looking around the house.

"Thanks," I smiled.

"How well did you know Marsh?"

"I knew him very well," I answered.

"Where did he go? Where is he?" the officer asked.

Wanting to answer the question in a thoughtful way, I said, "He is in a better place with his creator."

"No, his body was found on the shore," he said, sipping his coffee.

"No, it can't be. It has to be a mistake," I told the officer.

"There was positive ID found on him, same blood type, and several lacerations and stab wounds were on his body."

"This has to be a setup by Josalynn," I said vehemently.

"You have the right to your opinions. We have checked your records and you have no violations against you. You also helped Marsh get his life together. His records are also clean. There was no reason for anyone to kill him. Josalynn has a lot of things against her, many files at the precinct, and that is why we are doing extra investigation on this specific matter," the officer said, finishing his coffee.

"It might be the man who used to own this house. He was never found," I informed him.

"I will look into it," he answered, standing and shaking my hand.

"I would appreciate that," I answered, escorting him down the stairs to the beach. I watched him until he disappeared behind a dune. I ran my fingers through my disheveled hair, rubbed my face, and kicked my feet through the sand. This was not what I had anticipated this morning. My peaceful coexistence at this house was turning into turmoil. I chugged my coffee and went back upstairs to the deck. I sat in a chair and smacked my wrist on the handles. The squeak of the sliding door startled me.

"Is everything okay?" Marcus asked, sitting on the deck.

"Not really," I answered honestly.

"Do you want to talk about it?"

I remained silent for a moment to get my thoughts together and spat out, "That bitch Josalynn is trying to drive me crazy."

"What did she do this time?" he asked angrily.

"The officer claimed that the dead body on the shore was Marsh."

"That is insane!"

"They are investigating this matter because they don't believe her. I have to hope for the best. Why is she doing this?"

"Just remain calm and don't let her get to you."

I took a deep breath and clamed down. "You are right. Sometimes I let things get to me without knowing the final outcome. I am glad I have you here to calm me down," I told him seriously.

"I am going to go and talk to her."

"No, you can't. It will only make things worse," I begged.

Suddenly a scent of perfume filled the air. I looked over the railing and saw an unfamiliar woman below. She looked at me and climbed the steps to the deck. I approached her and wondered who she was.

"Hello, I am Katy Lane," she smiled.

"I am Joah."

"The house looks wonderful," she said, looking around the premises.

Marcus excused himself and left.

Katy circled the deck and seemed to be in a daze. She pushed her fingers through her long blond hair, closed her eyes, and took a deep breath. "It's just like I remembered," she said, looking at me.

"Who are you?" I wondered, totally confused.

"I used to live here with my husband," she said, leaning against the railing.

I took a deep breath and sat down. "Wow, I never expected this," I told her.

"I am sorry for intruding on you. I had to see the house one more time," she said, breathing in the sea air.

"What brings you to this house?"

Katy sat on a deck chair, covered her face with her arms, and took a moment to think. "My husband and I were very happy here for a long time. He loved it here. I could not handle the loneliness and being away from my family. I finally left him one day."

"I am so sorry," I said sympathetically.

"I begged him to come to New York and to leave this place. He would not listen to me," she said, rekindling the past.

I motioned for her to continue.

Katy grasped the seashell beads around her neck. "He wanted me to come back and so many times I wanted to, but I could not do it. I could not stand another single day on this beach. Doug was a dreamer and loved to walk along the beaches, fish, camp, and investigate the island. He did a lot of research on fish oils to find cures for certain diseases; he was an oceanographer. I was mortified when I found out about his disappearance."

"When was the last time you heard from him?"

Katy thought for a moment and fidgeted in her chair. "Right after the hurricane. He was devastated by the destruction of the house. He would send me e-mails and letters regularly and then nothing. The authorities informed me that he had disappeared. I did not want to think about it and wanted to block this house from my mind."

"Is that why you never informed the real estate authorities about this house?"

"Yes, I did not want it. It was Doug's place not mine, and his insurance covered the costs of the house. I just abandoned it," she wept.

"Why are you here?" I wondered.

"I just want closure and to know what really happened to Doug," Katy said, wiping her tear-drenched eyes with a cloth.

"And how do you intend to find closure?" I asked curiously.

"There was a body found on the beach nearby and I thought that it might be him. It would be wonderful to just look at him one more time," she said, looking out to sea.

"They think it is Marsh, a friend of mine, and I think they are wrong," I said, sharing my information with her.

"I know they are wrong," Katy replied, turning to face me.

"How do you know?" I asked curiously.

"There was also a ring on his finger with a dolphin. It was his favorite. Joah, it is my husband," she said, struggling to hold back her tears. "There is no doubt in my mind. I should be happy that I have closure, but the stabs and lacerations are troubling me. He was well liked and admired by everyone."

"What about the clothes he was wearing?"

"I talked to the coroners. Doug always wore specific colors and materials. He would not be caught dead in the clothes he was wearing."

"Do you think it is foul play?"

Katy stood up and guffawed. "I don't trust that woman Josalynn who found him. I believe she planned this entire thing to get back at you. That is why I am here. I want to prove that she is a fake and a liar. I don't think she expected me to be in the picture," she said, circling the deck.

"I am glad that you are in the picture," I smiled.

"May I see the rest of the house?" she asked anxiously.

"Yes, be my guest," I answered, opening the sliding door and showing her into the corridor. Katy acted like she was in a daze as she looked through the windows, touched the wooden cabinets and tables, and ran her hands over the railing of the spiral staircase. Her face was aglow and she smiled from ear to ear. "I loved him so much, yet I could not be with him or have him," she blubbered.

"I wish there was something I could do to help you."

"There is," she said, holding back her tears.

I waited to hear her response.

"My senses tell me that you are a beautiful person with good intentions for others. I want you to have this house and continue helping others Never give up your dreams," she told me as she turned to leave.

I followed her to the deck and stood beside her.

"Don't worry about anything and continue what you are doing. Is that a promise?" she asked, waiting for my response.

"You better believe it," I answered excitedly.

"That is what I like to hear," she said as though she were going to fly. The wind brushed through her clothes and made her appear like a ballon in her sleek outfit. She was a very attractive woman with warm features, a thin body, and a nice smile. She tossed her hair into the breeze as she proceeded toward the boat dock. Katy sat on a wooden bench with her legs crossed and motioned for me to sit next to her. She rummaged through her purse and handed me a card. "This is where I will be staying, the Tigris Hotel on the mainland. If you need me, please contact me immediately."

"Thanks so much," I said, stashing the card in my wallet.

"No problem," she smiled, closing her purse.

"How could anyone let a beautiful woman like you go?" I asked, gawking.

She thought for a moment and licked her lips. "The same as you letting me go now."

"What do you mean?" I asked, confused.

"You have your work to do on this earth and I would be nothing but a burden for you, the same as I was for Doug," she said sadly.

"Katy, you have been such a big help for me and have relieved my anxiety and stress."

"Yes, and seeing this house and bringing back the past have also helped me," she said, ears alerted

The chugging of a boat engine and the blurting of a whistle echoed in the distance.

"How did you know the boat was coming? Are you a psychic?" I asked, astonished.

"No, no," she laughed. "After living here for so many years, I can feel the vibration and see the movement of the water."

The ferryboat pulled into place and anchored.

"That is remarkable," I said, helping her onto the dock.

"Joah, it was so nice meeting you. I want everything to be finalized and this house turned over to you. I was hoping that someone like you would take over and take care of this place."

"This means a lot to me," I said, hardly able to speak.

She kissed my cheek and proceeded over the plank. I watched her as she found a seat and waved. I was so mesmerized that I didn't even see Colin getting off the boat. He gawked at me, waved his umbrella, and smacked my leg with his briefcase. "Ouch!" I jumped.

"Who is she? She is beautiful."

"Her name is Katy," I said, rubbing my knee.

The ferryboat left the pier and headed out to sea.

"What was she doing here?"

"She used to live here with her husband," I told him, stepping from the dock to the beach.

"Oh, no, does she want the house back?" he asked, hoping he was wrong.

"No, she does not want the house. She wants me to have it," I told him, helping him with his things.

Colin kicked through the sand with his sandals and scraped the crystals from his hairy legs. "Why does there have to be sand on beaches?"

"Why are there cement sidewalks and roads in the city?" I shrugged.

"I guess you are right," he answered, climbing the stairs to the deck.

"What brings you here?" I wondered.

"I heard about the body found on the beach. It scared me. The newspapers said it might be Marsh, but I had to know for sure that it was not you and that you were okay."

"I am fine," I told him, following behind.

"Was it Marsh?"

"No, I think it was Katy's husband. That is why she was here. He was lost several months ago," I said, placing his things inside.

Colin set up his umbrella and sat beneath it to avoid the sun. "I bet you were concerned when you heard it might be Marsh."

"Yes, I was very worried," I said, taking a seat next to him.

"I knew there had to be something wrong. If you were not ready to go to the other side, it would not accept you."

"Yes, you know that as well as I do," I said, facing Colin.

"I don't know why I am so afraid of death and dying," he muttered.

"Colin, you were my first try. Maybe you should try again."

"No, I am not ready to go. I don't like living here, but I can't do anything for myself. I am a sorry lot, afraid of everything," he confessed.

"Would you like a soda?" I asked.

Colin nodded and fumbled with his umbrella to block the sun.

I handed him a soda and got one for myself.

Colin sipped the cool liquid. "What is going on with Marcus?"

"He is ready to go, but he needs to have forgiveness within himself. He blames himself for what happened between him and Josalynn."

"Marcus and Josalynn were once together?" he asked, surprised.

"Yes, I just found out myself. She is his ex-girlfriend," I told him, nodding and sipping the soda.

"That is so odd. They are both so different," Colin commented, rummaging through his black bag.

"Yep, I thought the same thing," I said, finishing my soda.

"Listen, I brought some new frames for Mum's pictures taken at the farewell party and I want to place the photos in them and put them on the walls and tables," he said, pulling things out of his black bag.

"That sounds like a good idea," I told him, startled by squeaky steps. I turned and saw Marcus walking toward me. Colin left the deck and went into the house.

"Who was the pretty lady?" Marcus winked, sitting.

"She used to live in this house with her husband," I told him.

"Wow, why did she come back?"

"She is looking for closure. She left her husband years ago. She did not like the loneliness and missed her family, so she left him. She wanted him to come back, but he preferred to stay here and finish his work as an oceanographer," I informed him.

"What happened to her husband?"

"He was lost after the storm and no one could find him. She was hoping that the dead body found on the shore was him."

"Does she want the house back?"

"No, she has agreed to give me the house. She wants no part of it."

"That is wonderful," he smiled, smacking my arm.

"Did you talk to Josalynn?" I wondered.

"Yes, I did," he answered, lowering his head and thinking.

"What is on your mind?" I asked, sensing his sudden distance.

"I have been able to forgive Josalynn and I feel good about it. The lock that has been around my neck for so long is finally released.

"I am glad to hear that," I smiled.

"I still have this fear of going to the other side. I don't want to end up like Marsh as a dead body."

"This is her hold on you to keep you from going," I informed him.

"Well, it is a strong hold," he shivered.

"She does not want you to leave and have eternal happiness because she can't have it. I do believe the dead body is Doug, the husband of Katy, the woman who used to own this house, and it will be clarified in time," I said positively.

"I hope you are right. I don't want to go to the other side until all of the investigation is finalized."

"I don't blame you. I would feel the same way," I agreed.

"I was really prepared to go until all of this happened," he said, standing and pacing the deck.

"You know that your disbelief will prevent you from going."

"I know that," he answered sadly.

"Don't let it stop you," Colin muttered, stepping onto the deck.

Marcus jumped and turned around. "I didn't know you were here."

"Yes, I am just working on some prints and frames."

"Your work is incredible. The pictures match the frames so perfectly. I enjoy looking at all of them," he smiled, turning toward him.

"Thanks, I enjoy doing them. It is my gift," he answered.

"What other gifts do you possess?" he asked.

"A special gift I wish I did have is to leave this earth without fear."

It all clicked together and Marcus understood. "You were the one who could not go to the other side because of disbelief."

"Yes, that is exactly right," he said, joining us.

"You were the first one to try," Marcus said, lighting a cigarette.

"Yes, but I am afraid of so many things in this world. I could never commit suicide because I would chicken out. I depend on my medication to stabilize my metabolism and I often have anxiety attacks."

I listened and was amazed by their conversation.

"What a horrible way to live," he said, puffing on his cigarette.

"Don't be like me. You have a chance to be free of your seizures and to live a normal life in the hereafter," Colin said, fumbling with a picture frame.

"Yes, you are right. I should take advantage of the situation."

Colin stood up and held a picture of Marsh. "I know he is in a better place and the dead body is someone else. I was with Joah all of the times the victims went to the other side. I was in the Realm Incarnate and it does exist," he said truthfully.

"Colin, I understand what you are saying and I appreciate your concern, but I have to be certain," he said, crushing the cigarette into an ashtray.

"Just take advantage of a good situation," Colin answered, exiting into the house.

Marcus leaned against the railing and looked out to sea.

"Just take your time until you are ready," I told him.

"Thanks for being so patient with me," he answered, turning to face me.

I placed my arm on his shoulder to reassure him that I understood. We left the deck and went into the house. I made a pot roast with carrots and mashed potatoes and we enjoyed the meal. Colin helped with the dishes and left around dusk. Marcus fell asleep on the couch watching a movie. Suddenly the lights flickered off. I went onto the deck beneath a protective porch to watch the storm. Thunder and lightning pounded in the sky, a sudden wind began to scatter debris everywhere, and raindrops fell onto my face. Palm tree branches bent and twisted, creaked and whistled, and broke and fell to the ground. Large brush crackled and crunched. A blast of sand was tossed into the air. The ocean waves roared and formed a mist into the air. I sat in silence and shivered. Marcus awoke and went to bed. I remained on the deck for a while until the rain stopped and restarted the generator. The lights flickered back on. I later went to bed listening to the rhythm of the rain.

The next day I awoke to a cool and sunny morning. There was freshly brewed coffee, but Marcus was not home. A sudden knock on the sliding door startled me. A man and a woman were vivid through the glass. I opened the door to greet them.

"Hello, Joah," the lady smiled.

I recognized her immediately as Katy, but the gentleman was not familiar.

"This is my attorney, Mr. Lomas, and I want to finalize the papers. I tried calling you yesterday night, but your electricity must have been off because of the storm."

"Why is he here?" I wondered.

"I want to finalize the sale of this house to you. I want it to be legalized."

"That will be fine," I said, drying off the deck chairs with a rag. There was a lot on my mind and I was not ready for company. I was wearing an old T-shirt and boxers. I fumbled with my hair to try to fix it.

Mr. Lomas fumbled with some papers and handed them to Katy. He scratched his bald head and gray beard. There were a lot of forms to sign dealing with ownership, finances, taxes, and fees. Most of the funds were covered by Katy and her husband's insurance. It was giving me a headache. I tossed the papers aside and looked at both of them. "Katy, what about your husband?"

She looked at me strangely. "He is dead."

"I know that. What about the body found on the shore?"

Her face was filled with concern. "You were not notified yet?"

"No, not at all," I told her.

"The dead body found on the shore was my husband."

"Oh, that is a relief," I breathed.

"They are still concerned about the cuts and lacerations, but they think they were from sharp coral and rocks. I am surprised the police did not notify you."

"The storm did knock out my power, so that might be why."

"Anyway, let's continue with the rest of the paperwork. I want to make final arrangements for my husband and have closure. This will mean a lot to me," she answered, trying to rush things along.

I continued filling out forms as Mr. Lomas explained each item with clarity and distinction. It took another hour before everything was finalized. Once it was all complete, we sat and relaxed. We all enjoyed coffee and sweet rolls.

Katy paced the deck with her cup of coffee. "I really did love it here at one time," she said, looking at the ocean.

"What tore you away from it?" I asked, wondering.

"I began to hate and despise it because of Doug. He tore me away from its beauty."

"Why did you let him do this to you?" I asked, sipping my coffee.

"I did it to myself. I wanted him here with me, but he was always working, leaving me alone. I always sat on this deck by myself," she wept.

"Loneliness can do strange things to each individual."

"Yes, and one day I packed up my things and left him. I warned him so many times about how I was feeling and he refused to listen. I felt bad for a long time and he begged me to return, but I could not bear being alone," she said, wiping her tears.

"Did you love him?" I inquired.

She was silent for a moment while searching for words. "Yes, very much. That was why it hurt so much. I wanted to be with him, yet I could not stand his way of life. It was not what I wanted for myself," she answered, finishing her coffee.

Mr. Lomas finished organizing all of the paperwork and placed it in his briefcase. He nodded and stood up.

"I should be leaving. They are going to cremate what is left of Doug's remains and have closure. I will be leaving in a few days."Katy informed me.

"Thanks for everything. It has been wonderful meeting you."

"Please take good care of the house. You have done a wonderful job so far. Thanks for letting me reminisce," she said, kissing my cheek.

Mr. Lomas shook my hand and I escorted them to the pier. The ferryboat arrived in a few minutes and they boarded it and left. I was so busy watching them that I did not realize Officer Jenkins was standing in front of me. I jumped and looked at him. He scratched his bald head with a blank stare like I was crazy. There was a brief silence until I said, "What brings you here?"

"Do you have a few minutes to talk?"

"Yes, just follow me to the house," I said, leading.

"I am sorry for not informing you about my visit, but your phone was not working. I thought I would take a chance to see if you were home."

"That is fine," I said, showing him to a seat on the deck.

"I noticed Katy Lane and her lawyer leaving. Did they talk to you?," the officer said, sitting.

"Yes, she informed me that the person found was her husband, Doug."

"Yes, that is correct," he answered.

"That is great news," I said, taking a seat across from him.

He lowered his head in deep thought and said, "There is more to it."

"Tell me," I said, not sure if I wanted to know.

"The body is definitely Katy's husband. The blood samples on the shirt were from Marsh, planted on the body by Josalynn, but the bones and flesh were definitely Katy's husband's."

"So what is the problem?"

Officer Jenkins took a deep breath and said, "We are still concerned about the cuts and lacerations. The body should have deteriorated more than it did."

"And what does that mean?"

"Someone was preserving the body."

I was stunned without words.

"The story goes that he was killed in the hurricane, but others have said they had seen him after the storm. They claim he was devastated by the destruction of the house."

"Do you think he committed suicide?"

"That could be, but ..." he paused.

I waited for him to continue.

"We are not ruling out suicide"

"What about the cuts and lacerations? These could not have been done by him because of their location and impossibility of reaching."I suggested.

That is why I need your help. Let me know anything you hear. Katy seems to like you and might open up to you," he said, fidgeting.

"I will do that," I told him.

Office Jenkins nodded and turned toward me. "You seem like a mature and descent human being."

"Thanks, I am," I told him.

"Why are you dealing with the hereafter?" he spat out.

"That is a gift given to me," I said.

"It is a gift that could lead you to prison," he informed me.

"I am doing nothing wrong. I have papers and written documents of everything I do. I can show them to you. Everyone has free will to make their own decisions," I answered sincerely.

"There are a lot of skeptics out there who might not think the same way. Many of them are saying that you are taking their money and lives and using them for your own good," he said, gritting his teeth.

"I would never hurt or harm anyone. I am here to help others."

"They also say that you are sick and diseased."

"Yes, but I am getting better."

"They also say that you are gay."

"That is not true," I snapped.

The officer slowed down and leaned against his chair. "I am just telling you what others are proclaiming. Keep your nose clean," he said, leaving.

Sweat beaded on my forehead. I felt mesmerized and numb. The dampness formed ice crystals, freezing me to the seat. I thought that everything was solved and finished, yet it had just begun. The sun played over my body and melted the extreme chill. I came back to life when Marcus ran up the stairs to join me. "I just saw the officer. Are you okay?"

"Yes, I think I am," I trembled.

"What happened? You look startled."

I brushed my fingers through my hair and was uncertain where to begin. I took a few moments to get my thoughts together.

"Why are you still in your torn tank top and boxers?"

"It is a long story," I told him, fixing myself another cup of coffee.

"I will tell you what I know," he said, pouring himself a cup of brew.

"Tell me," I said, sitting and sipping.

"I went to talk to Josalynn and mentioned nothing about you."

I choked on the coffee and wiped my mouth.

"She told me that the person found on the shore was not Marsh but the owner of this house," he informed me.

"That is correct. I talked to Katy Lane this morning. She is going to have him cremated."

"Wow, you had a lot of visitors. Anyway, they are accusing Josalynn of placing blood and the clothes of another person on the body."

"Go on," I said, urging him to continue.

"She refuses to believe any of it and denies everything. She told the police that they should be honored that she called them when she discovered the remains on the beach, like she was doing them a favor," Marcus laughed.

"It sounds like her," I guffawed.

"The best part is that I am no longer afraid. I am ready to go to the other side."

"That is wonderful," I smiled, sipping and drinking the java.

"Josalynn has proved to me how conniving and deceptive she can be. I don't want to have anything to do with her. I have forgiven her and hold no hurt or pain within my heart. I should have trusted you from the start," he proclaimed, chugging his coffee.

"That is really nice to know," I said, smacking his shoulder.

"I feel so good," Marcus said, moving on the deck.

I laughed as he twisted and turned, making his own dance performance.

"Now let me tell you want I know," I said, giggling.

His dance debut ended and he sat down.

"This house has been legally signed over to me. I am the new owner," I chuckled.

"That is wonderful news. When did this occur?"

"This morning Katy Lane came over with her attorney to finalize all of the paperwork," I told him, showing him the forms.

"Wow, this is great. You have had a really busy morning," he said, examining the documents.

"There is more," I informed him.

He handed me the papers and urged me to continue.

"Officer Jenkins told me that the remains found on the beach definitely are Doug Lane's, but there are some uncertainties."

"What might that be?" he wondered.

"The body seems to be too preserved and the cuts are not from rocks or coral."

"That is really odd," Marcus commented.

"Maybe Katy or Josalynn had something to do with it. Josalynn is definitely a suspect since she planted false clothes and blood on the body. That was not very smart of her."

"You know she did that just to keep me from going to the other side. Josalynn likes to have total control of everything. That is her domain. She knows she can no longer control me, but that does not mean she will quit trying. She has no other choice," Marcus said, reassuring me.

"It is nice to see you with a positive attitude," I said pleasantly.

"You and I have to work out plans for my departure to the other side. I have a lot to do to get myself ready. I want to live in a world without seizures," he told me, leaving his seat and going inside. It was nice to see Marcus so overjoyed, happy, and content. I wish I felt the same way. I was happy to see him go, yet it would mean the loss of another friend. I knew there would be others who would need my help and assistance, yet they would leave just like everyone else. Maybe I needed something more permanent in my life. I needed someone to remain with me for a while. I was not strong enough to live alone. This was clear to me after Marcus went to the other side.

The Mourning After the Storm
Chapter Five

I spent the next few days going to Craters Peak, my old home town, and decided to attend Saint John's Episcopal Church. It was a promise I had made to Father Leonard and Colin months ago and I enjoyed being in the presence of my creator. It was a beautiful church adorned with stained glass windows and a tall rounded corridor. There were large wooden doors that led into the corridor. A smell of incense filled the air as I sat in a pew toward the back of the church. Beautiful terracotta statues and pictures were scattered throughout the vestibule. The altars were adorned with satin cloths and beautiful flowers and there were lit candles all around them. The fiery lights reflected over the large statues. I was always early for services and just sat silently in a pew thinking. There were so many puzzling things facing me and I was not coming up with any logical answers.

"You have been spending a lot of time in church," a familiar voice echoed through the chambers.

"I just need time to pray," I jumped.

"How have you been coping with things?" Father Leonard inquired, sitting next to me.

"Not real well. I just can't get over this. Why did this happen the way it did? It does not make any sense."

"Each of our lives is planned. We have no say as to when we live or die," he told me.

"We were so close," I cried hysterically.

Father Leonard sat in silence and didn't respond.

"When you and Colin came to the island, I was numbed. I had saved Marcus's life once, why not again?" I sighed, looking for an answer.

"I wish I could answer you," Father Leonard said as he bowed his head. "You had to save yourself. Your life was spared to help others. You can't blame yourself for what happened."

"But I do. I do," I wept.

Father Leonard sat and sympathized with me until he had to leave to prepare for the afternoon services. Colin came to join me.

"I never thanked you for coming to rescue me after the storm," I said, turning toward him.

"It would kill me to lose you," he said, teary eyed.

"That is so nice to know," I said, hugging him.

"When are you planning on going back to the house?"

His question caught me off guard. It was something very painful for me to understand, yet it was something I had to face. I left Colin, walked to the altar, and knelt down. The last day with Marcus played over and over again in my mind.

Everything was planned for his departure to the other side. There were several of his friends and family, and they gathered at the house for the eulogy. Father Leonard gave a wonderful sermon and everyone was impressed by his kind words and scriptures.

Marcus wanted everyone to be together for his final meal. There was a buffet prepared with plenty of fruits, rigatoni in a meat sauce, green beans, and assorted cookies. It all smelt so good. I fixed myself a plate of the scrumptious food and sat alone at a table.

"It looks good," a familiar voice spoke out.

I looked up and saw Josalynn glaring at me.

"May I join you?" she asked.

Though I was not in the mood to see her, I nodded, "Be my guest."

She pulled up a chair and placed her plate of food and drink on the table. "I know you must not be very fond of me right now."

"You guessed right," I said, munching.

"You have to understand where I am coming from. You have hurt me very much," she said, sitting.

"I understand that you are conniving, deceitful, and revengeful."

"Those are harsh words," she said, opening her can of soda.

"How can you even be here after trying to deceive Marcus and preventing him from being free? You refused to let him forgive you, and then you tried to make others think the dead body was Marsh."

"It was very wrong of me," she confessed.

"Yet you have the guts to be here," I said, smacking my fork on the table.

"Please don't be upset with me," she begged.

I exhaled and calmed down.

"You have taken a lot from me. Marsh would come to visit me and he was actually going to move in with me, but he met you and wanted to be with you hoping something would happen. I also wanted you and was attracted to you. I always get what I want," she told me.

"This was beyond my control. I did not plan any of this."

"I know you didn't," she said, eating some of her food.

"Why are you here?"

She tossed her long dark hair into the breeze, folded her legs, and leaned against the chair. "I wanted to be here for Marcus."

"And a week ago you tried to confuse him by making me look like a fraud," I snapped.

"I was not ready to let him go," she said honestly.

"You are a very confusing woman," I said, finishing my food.

"Even though things did not work out for us, I liked having him around and talking to him."

"I do too, but I know he will be better off in another place and won't have to suffer so much. I am willing to let him go."

"I am too," she said sheepishly.

"I don't believe you," I told her, leaving the table.

"I believe you. Maybe I am jealous of your powers," she confessed, trying to stop me.

It was obvious that she wanted something from me by trying to be so benevolent and trustworthy. "I have a job to do."

"May I come with you to the Realm Incarnate?" she begged.

"No, you have caused enough problems. I only take the person going to the other side with me," I informed her.

"Can't you make an exception?" she wondered, flaunting.

"There is no end to your deceit, is there," I said, walking away from her and ending our conversation.

It was close to the final hour. I got the boat ready to go to the small island where the Realm Incarnate was located. The motor was working and the boat was full of gas. The seats were cushioned and comfy. Everything was set and ready to go.

A sudden drop fell on my face, but I was not sure if it was rain, a mist, or ocean drizzle. The sky was cloudy but there was plenty of sunshine.

He looked very handsome dressed in a striped suit, white shirt, and dark-blue tie. His hair was cut and styled. Marcus pulled me aside to talk to me. There was a look of concern on his face. "Is something wrong?" I asked.

He bit his lip and seemed anxious. "Can Josalynn come with us?" he asked.

"Absolutely not," I answered.

"I know this is against the rules. Joah, I want her to be there with me."

Glancing into his eyes, I knew I could not stand in his way. "Yes, yes, and tell her she can go."

"Joah, thanks so much," he said excitedly, rushing to tell her.

We boarded the boat, Josalynn and Marcus on one end, and I sat toward the front to start the engine and drive the boat. Marcus gave his final farewells to his loved ones as we sped away. I drove the boat over the large waves and headed toward the small island. It seemed to be getting cloudier as we sped toward the Realm Incarnate.

A look of concern covered his face as he clung to the seat.

"I am not used to the wavy water," Marcus said dizzily.

"Just some rough water. Nothing to worry about," I said, trying to console him.

"I wish I could swim. Being out here in the middle of nowhere frightens me," Josalynn trembled.

"I am a good swimmer, so don't worry," I reassured them.

"I don't know if I like this," he said, leaning over the side of the boat and puking.

Josalynn covered her face and looked away from him. She was also getting seasick.

This sudden storm was worrying me. A large wave flung the boat into the air and tossed it in a circular motion, twisting and turning it like a top. A gusty wind plowed against it. Thunder pounded in the sky and lightning hissed over the horizon. Rain fell heavily and filled the boat. We struggled to get rid of the excess water, but it seemed like a worthless task. I tried to keep the boat afloat. Nothing seemed to be working as the waves engulfed the boat and flipped it over. I lost sight of them as they submerged beneath the water. I bobbed through the waves looking for them and reaching for them, but I could not locate them. The rain, fog, and mist made it impossible to see anything. Water was filling my lungs, choking me, and I knew if I continued the search, I would drown. I saw the island in the distance and swam toward it. It hurt me to give up my search for them. I swam with all of my might to save myself. I collapsed on the shore and coughed up water and sand. I sat in the rain hoping to see them floating or swimming to shore. The storm ended and I was alone.

I was tired of mourning and being alone. I had been sleeping in a tent near the Realm Incarnate for about a week. I just wanted to see Marcus one more time to tell him I was sorry that I could not save his life. It was not going to happen and I had to move on with my life.

I left the altar and approached Colin. "I am going back home today."

"That is wonderful," he exclaimed joyfully.

"I had saved Marcus's life once and I think he knows that I care."

"Good for you."

"I am not staying for services," I said excitedly.

"That is okay. I will tell Father Leonard."

"I appreciate that very much," I said, walking away.

"Don't forget to pick up those frames at the novelty shop," Colin said, reminding me.

I waved and exited the church.

I took a ferryboat back to Padre Island and another boat to my house. Then I strolled the beach to my small boat on the shore. I started the engine and drove to the small island where I had been staying for about a week. I gathered up my tent, sleeping bag, and other supplies, cleaned up the premises, and loaded everything onto the boat. It was time to go home. I drove the boat to my dock at the house, unloaded everything, and placed it on the deck. I walked to the mainland and through town and stood in front of the senior home where Mum once lived. She was gone, Marsh was gone, and now Marcus and Josalynn were on the other side. I was angry at the way things turned out, yet I knew they were in a better place. I passed by a novelty shop along the boardwalk, the one Colin always patronized and recalled he had asked me to pick up a few wooden frames for him. He wanted to place photos taken during the final farewell into them. The front doors squeaked as I stepped into the corridor. Trails of dust, dirt, and webs hung from the ceiling. The front desk was covered with portraits of musicians, movie stars, and starlets. A fan hummed and buzzed above me and seemed like it was going to fall from the roof. A stench of dampness and sewage filled the air. I wondered why Colin would even come to this place. I looked at pictures of movie stars scattered around the walls and windows and recognized a few of them.

A woman with pitch-black hair and tattoos approached me and muttered with a mouthful of gum, "May I help you?"

"Yes, I am here to pick up a few frames for Colin Mustfred, a good friend of mine. Here is the receipt," I said, handing it to her.

She examined it and went to the back room.

I leaned against the desk and noticed a young guy with blond hair and a small goatee rummaging through a load of pictures in a box. Some of them looked familiar. He glared at me as I neared him. Many of them looked exactly like the ones Colin had done for me. The guy looked bewildered, scared, and sweat beaded on his brow. "Where did you get these?" I asked, eyeing them. I lifted my head and he jolted out of the store. I was a quick runner and chased him down the street, across an alley, and through a parking lot. I thought I had lost him and circled a fence where he was hiding. He tossed over a few trash cans to stop me. I jumped over them, ran beneath a low overhang beneath an underpass, and caught up to him. I grabbed his legs, knocked him over, and pounded his chest.

"Please don't damage my face," he begged.

"Where the hell did you get those framed pictures?" I screamed, waiting for an answer.

"They were given to me by a friend," he trembled, blocking my punch.

"That is not the answer I am looking for," I said, clenching my fist.

He blocked my punch again and squirmed.

"Are you some kind of lunatic?" he spat.

"Why did you run away from me?"

"You looked like you wanted to steal my pictures," he told me.

"And who did you steal the pictures from?" I yelled, slapping his face.

"Get off of me," he grunted.

"Not until you tell the truth," I told him, waiting.

"All right, all right, you win. I stole them from a dude's house. I thought the house was vacant or boarded up. It was dark for days," he confessed.

"It was my house. Those pictures were given to me by a special friend. They mean a lot to me and I want them back. If I release you, you are coming with me to get them."

"And then what are you going to do to me?" he shuddered.

"I should turn you over to the police, but if you come quietly, nothing will happen."

"How do I know you are not just bluffing?"

"It is either that or I beat the shit out of you right now!"

The guy calmed down, took a deep breath, and relaxed.

I released him, stood up, and glared at him. "Who put you up to this? Why did you rob my place?"

He slowly stood up and brushed dirt from his clothes. His eyes were glued to me. It looked like he wanted to dart away, but he knew he had no chance against me. "A guy named Marsh. He told me that you had a lot of valuable things."

"How did you know Marsh?" I asked, surprised.

"He used to hang out with me and get me drugs, but then he reformed and went to another place. I guess you were the prophet who sent him," he spat out.

"Yes, were you at the eulogy?"

"No, he wanted me to come, but I couldn't go. I didn't want to go."

"He never told me anything about you," I told him.

"We were just acquaintances. I don't get close to anyone. I have gotten into so many problems with the law. Please don't turn me in."

"I told you I wouldn't as long as I get all of my things back."

"That is going to be a problem. Some of the things I stole from you have already been sold," he shuddered.

"Are most of the photos still there?" I hoped, walking forward.

"Yes, they are all at the store," he said, following me.

"That is good. They hold a lot of special remembrances of friends for me."

I don't have any friends," he confessed.

"How long did you know Marsh?"

"I knew him about a year. He was an odd and scary character."

"What do you mean?" I asked, crossing a street.

"He was very fickle He was planning on driving to California and even purchased a car. He kept calling for his registration and license and then decided to take a train. He would hide from the sun and swim in the rain."

"Yes, that is so true. I didn't know he was planning on changing his mind about going to the other side," I said sadly.

"Everyone has doubts. It was during the time he first met you. I would feel the same way if someone told me that I could leave the earth without having to die," he answered, moving ahead of me.

"Who are you?" I inquired, walking faster.

He began to speak and suddenly took off. He twisted and turned, ducked down an alley, and ran as fast as he could. I chased him for a while and let him go. It was not worth wasting my time with him. I walked back to the novelty store and went to the front desk.

"Where did you go?" the woman with the tattoos asked, handing me a box of frames.

"I just saw an old friend," I told her.

She leaned forward to display her large breasts. "His name is Marty. He is a problem child with no family. The police are always looking for him," she laughed.

"Where does he live?"

"Wherever," she said, tossing her arms into the air.

"Listen, this bag of framed photos is not for sale," I told her.

"Are they yours?" she wondered.

"Yes, they belong to me," I told her.

"So I guess Marty robbed your house and you are not pressing charges," she said, looking at the objects.

"He took off and I lost him," I informed her.

"He does this all of the time. He is very sneaky and tricky," she said, blowing a bubble and popping it.

"I found that out. Thanks for all of your info," I said, grabbing my things and exiting the shop.

"My pleasure," she smiled, going to the back room.

Usually I would walk home, but I took the ferryboat taxi to the house since I had so many bags of things to carry. It was a pleasant afternoon with light breezes and plenty of sunshine. I looked over the railing and noticed a reflection of my face in the clear water. My skin was very dry and my hair and facial hair were coarse. It seemed like years had gone by. The whistle sounded and I saw my house in the distance. I grabbed my things and waved to the driver, stepped onto the pier, and walked across the dock.

"Help me!" a voice echoed below.

I dropped my bags and looked around the dock. I could not see anything through the holes in the floor of the dock. I circled the pier and noticed someone clinging to a wooden support.

"Over here," the voice cried, slapping his fists in the rippling water.

"What happened?" I called.

"My foot fell through a loose board and it is trapped. I can't move it."

The voice was not familiar. I looked at the blond-haired guy and knew immediately it was Marty.

"I don't blame you for just leaving me here. I deserve it since I am such a loser," he said, looking up at me.

I was more concerned about saving him. There was a supply box on the dock and I got a hammer, rope, and a small saw. I lowered myself onto a cement post holding the wooden supports and balanced myself. It was difficult to see how his leg was jammed with the rippling water twirling over it. I ripped the lower part of his pants and looked at his leg. It was bleeding and cut from splintered boards and nails. I struggled to grasp the rotted boards, loosen them with the hammer, and cut them with the saw. I was very careful not to hurt his foot. I removed several nails and chipped boards and freed his leg from the hole.

Fear covered his face and sweat beaded on his brow as he saw his injured leg. He looked like he was going to pass out from the blood.

He turned to the side and vomited. "I am so sorry," he apologized, wiping slop from his mouth.

I tossed water over his wounds to wash off the blood. Marty was just a child and it was sad to see a young guy in so much turmoil. I helped him to the top of the dock and let him rest on a wooden seat. I put the supplies away and walked toward him. "How did this happen?"

"I stowed away on the ferryboat in a large wooden box and jumped from it and swam to your dock. I was going to hide beneath the pier until I was brave enough to face you. I fell through the boards and panicked," he explained.

"You are free to run away again," I told him.

"I have nowhere else to go," he wept.

"I can't believe that after robbing me, you have the guts to come to me for help."

"I apologize for making such a stupid mistake. I needed money to get my next high. I did not know who lived in this house. After I ran away from you, I felt so guilty. I have to do something with my life; I can't live like this forever. You are the first person who has been nice to me," he said sincerely.

"Let's go to the house and wash your wounded leg and put some ointment and bandages on it."

"I appreciate it," he said, limping.

I led the way up the wooden stairs and approached the front door with the bags of pictures. Marty stumbled up the stairs behind me. I unlocked the sliding door with the key and looked inside of the house. There was broken glass on the floor, furniture knocked over, and drawers with their items scattered all over. It was a terrible mess.

"I will help you put everything into place," Marty promised.

I looked into his troubled green eyes and was ready to smack him. I controlled my temper and walked past trails of debris.

"Joah, please don't be angry with me," he begged.

"How did you know my name?" I wondered.

"Marsh talked to me a lot about you," he said.

I took him into the bathroom and had him sit on the tub. I cleaned his hurt ankle and upper foot with warm, soapy water and placed ointment on the wounds. He squinted and gritted his teeth like a little boy. "Ouch," he grunted.

"It will only hurt for a short while."

"You must not tell anyone that I am staying here."

"Who said you are staying here?" I questioned him.

"The police will arrest me and take me to prison," he informed me.

"And then I will be arrested for hiding you. I don't think so."

"This will be the perfect hideaway. They will never suspect me being here."

"No, you are leaving this evening after I give you some food to eat."

"I am not hungry," he said, leaving the bathroom.

"When was the last time you had a decent meal?"

He thought for a moment and could not answer.

"You can organize everything you messed up while I am cooking. You should also stay off your feet for a while," I told him.

"Stop acting like my father," he jumped.

"Where are your parents?" I wondered.

"Dad is in prison and Mom took off years ago," he said, pacing.

"Where have you been living?"

"Mostly at shelters and churches or with the homeless," he said, sorting things on the floor back into the drawers.

"I hope you like pizza," I told him.

"What guy does not like pizza?" he laughed, licking his lips. Marty worked hard cleaning up the glass and papers and filled garbage cans full of debris. He straightened up drawers of dish towels and rags, cleaned and polished the counters, swept the floors and polished the streaked tiles, and emptied a lot of the junk into a dumpster alongside the house.

Marty continued placing pictures on the wall and wondered about many of them. "Who is this guy?" he inquired.

I turned to face him and looked at the photo. "That is Marcus. He wanted to go to the other side because of his seizures. He suffered with continuous outbursts."

"How long ago did he go?"

Tears welled up in my eyes as I placed sauce and cheeses on a pizza crust. "I met Marcus a few months ago. He had a seizure and was strewn on the beach. I gave him mouth to mouth and brought him back to life. He lived with me for a while to decide what he wanted to do."

"Did he go for therapy or get help with his seizures?"

"He did, yet nothing helped. They would have had to do extensive brain surgery that could have left him incoherent, and the recovery would have taken several months. He did not want to go through with it because of the risk," I said, placing the pizza into the oven.

"I am sure he is better on the other side," Marty commented, placing the photo on the wall.

"He never made it to the Realm Incarnate," I told him.

"What do you mean?" Marty wondered.

I thought about the horrible day and shivered, stuttering, "A horrible storm developed and knocked over the boat before we got to the Realm Incarnate. He drowned along with this woman," I told him, showing Marty her picture. "I stayed on the beach and mourned for them," I said, weeping.

"Man, I am so sorry. I feel so awful," he said sincerely.

"It was partly my fault. I should have been more observant of the weather report. I should have never let Josalynn go with us. I could have spared at least one life," I said, checking the pizza.

"Who was the woman?" Marty inquired.

"She was Marcus's ex-girlfriend. I was not fond of her or her actions. She caused me a lot of heartaches and problems. I wish she was still alive so I could know the truth about certain things. Some of the things she did were not very nice. I don't want to go into it right now."

"I feel so sad about robbing you," he said, placing the framed photo on the wall.

"You needed the money and knew nothing about me; I was just another victim," I said sadly.

"I am really sorry for hurting you," he apologized. "I know Marsh," he said, looking at another photo, "but who is this older woman?" he asked, dusting off the frame.

"Her name was Mum. She gave me a lot of the furniture in the house," I told him, pointing to all of the items.

"Why did she want to leave?" he inquired.

"She lost her husband months ago after being married for fifty years. She missed him very much and wanted to be with him," I told him, checking the pizza.

"That is a long time to be together. Most of my relationships have lasted less than a month. Where did you get all of the photos of the movie stars?" he asked, placing them on the wall.

"My best friend Colin loves the theater. Most of them are collectibles from New York City, which you must know because you sold a few of them."

A look of concern covered his face as he tried to reframe some of the photos. "I promise I will try to replace the ones I stole and sold."

"That would mean a lot to me. They are special to me because they were given to me by Colin. My biggest disappointment will be when he comes to the house and sees them missing."

Marty hid his face in shame as he continued to clean and dust the frames and placed them on walls, desks, and end tables. He cleaned the spotted glass and straightened up the knocked-over items.

"The pizza is ready," I called, taking it out of the oven and placing it on the counter top.

"It smells good," he said, eyeing it.

"Take a break and eat," I said, setting the table with napkins and silverware.

Marty set the cleaning supplies aside and emptied out the buckets of filthy water. He limped toward the table and placed several slices of pizza on a paper plate. He sat down and took a bite. "Delicious," he commented as he licked his lips.

"I am glad you like it," I said, passing a can of soda to him.

He popped the lid and took a swig of it, mumbling, "I promise to replace the items I stole from you."

I chomped on the pizza and nodded.

"I am leaving after I finish eating," he blurted out.

His quick decision caught me by surprise and I thought I heard wrong. "You're leaving?" I repeated.

"Yes," he answered, munching and slurping, wiping his mouth with a napkin.

"Why did you go through all of this turmoil? I am very confused."

"I don't blame you. I am a very confusing person," he said, leaving the table.

"Do you need food or clothes?" I asked, finishing my meal.

"No, you have done enough. Is there anything else you need done?"

"No, nothing else," I shrugged, wiping my mouth.

Marty opened the sliding door and stepped onto the wooden terrace.

"Are you sure you know what you are doing?"

"Yes, I have to go," he answered abruptly, dodging my glance.

"If you ever need anything, definitely come back," I told him, grabbing my stomach. Suddenly I began to feel nauseated and dizzy. I grasped onto the railing for support, waiting for the horrible feeling to pass. Sweat beaded on my forehead as I struggled to catch my breath.

Marty looked at me with concern. He twisted around me and touched and probed, waiting for a response.

He repeated the same words, "What is wrong? Are you okay?"

"I am fine," I answered, struggling to stand.

"Are you ill?" Marty inquired.

My vision and my thoughts suddenly became clearer. "Yes, this is something that occurs sporadically. I receive more strength each time I send someone to the other side. I lost an opportunity for more healing when Marcus and Josalynn drowned."

"I did not know any of this," he confessed.

"I did not expect you to know," I said, coming back to reality.

"Will you be okay?" he wondered.

"I will be fine," I said, motioning for him to go.

"Thanks for all your help," he said, limping down the wooden stairs to the beach. He took a quick left and disappeared behind a mound of dunes.

I went into the house and ate a few more pieces of pizza, wrapped up the leftovers, and placed them into the fridge. I sat in a lounge chair to relax and regain my strength. I said a few prayers until I was interrupted by a knock on the door. I thought that perhaps it was Marty returning, but it was an older couple. I looked at them and could hardly believe my eyes; it was Mom and Dad. As soon as I opened the sliding door, I embraced Mom and shook Dad's hand. Their eyes were watery as they looked at me. "Joah, it is so good to see you," they both said in repetition

"It is so nice to see both of you," I said with joyful tears.

"We expected the worst when we heard about the storm and the death of Marcus and Josalynn. Father

Leonard informed us about everything. We were so scared of losing you," she said, shaking.

"Yes, it was a scare for me also," I shivered.

"How have you been coping with everything?"

"It has been a struggle, but I am doing okay," I told them.

"We were going to come earlier, but Father Leonard informed us that you were mourning on a small island across the bay."

"That is true. I needed time alone to think."

"Why didn't you call us?"

Her question caught me off guard. It was something I should have thought about, and it was very thoughtless of me to not have called. I answered with sincerity and truth. "You might say I was in a coma, an illusion of disbelief, and it has taken me this long to face everything."

Mom looked into my eyes and hugged me. "Joah, please don't ever leave us in the dark again."

"I promise I won't," I said sincerely, showing them into the house.

"The place looks wonderful," Mom said, looking around the rooms. "You did a wonderful job. Where did you get all of the furniture?"

"A woman, Mum, gave it to me," I informed them, pointing to her picture.

"Who was she?"

"She was a compassionate woman who lost her husband. They were together for over fifty years. I sent her to the other side to be with him."

"I am surprised that there are not crowds of people wanting to leave this earth," she commented, looking at other photos.

"Mom, it is not that easy. You must be ready to let go of all material wealth and have a clear conscience and no doubts or else you cannot go."

"How have you been feeling?" Dad asked.

I hid the truth from my father so not to worry him "Good and bad. I lost a good chance to regain more strength when Marcus drowned."

"We are just glad you are okay," Mom answered tearfully.

"Would you like some pizza?" I asked.

"Oh, no, we just ate," they told me.

"Would you like something to drink, lemonade?" I asked.

"That sounds good, something cold and refreshing," Dad answered.

I fixed each of us a glass of the cold liquid and sat with them on the terrace. It was a warm and pleasant afternoon with light breezes. An aromatic scent of flowers filled the air. The ocean waves were noisy as they crashed on the shore.

"We were shocked to read the article about the dead body found on the beach," Mom said, sipping her drink.

"Yes, Josalynn tried to make others believe it was Marsh. It was Katy's ex-husband, Doug. They were the owners of this place, and she was here for closure."

"Does she want to move back into the house?"

"No, she gave me the rights to the property and is returning to New York."

"That is wonderful!" Mom exclaimed. "So this is your house."

"Yes, it is," I smiled.

"Why did she give it up?" Dad asked.

"It is a long story. I wish I knew the truth. All I know is what Josalynn told me before she died."

"Can you tell us about it?" Mom asked, probing.

"Yes, but I am not sure if it is the truth. That is why I wish Josalynn was still alive," I said, sipping.

Mom and Dad leaned back in anticipation of my story.

"Katy claims that she left the island because of loneliness. Her family was from New York and she wanted to be with them. Her husband was dedicated to his work as an oceanographer and he wanted to remain on this island."

"That makes sense," Mom commented.

"The story goes that Doug rented a puddle-jumper plane in the middle of winter to go to New York. He decided he wanted to be with her. Josalynn offered to go with him. There was a sudden turbulence in the air and the plane swerved from side to side, up and down, and twisted in a circular motion. The pilot struggled to mobilize the plane. Josalynn stayed in the cockpit while Doug went to check the baggage area for loose objects and security."

Mom and Dad sat in silence with their mouths wide open waiting to hear the conclusion.

"There was a loud whooshing sound and the jiggling of a door. Josalynn went to investigate and was sucked into the baggage compartment. Luckily, the emergency door automatically closed. She grabbed onto some hooks for support. The freezing air made it difficult for her to hold on. The utility door had come ajar and filled the compartment with frigid air. Her eyes were blinded as she felt her way to the lever that would release the latch and lock it. It seemed like hours of searching and feeling until she finally reached the emergency release. The door closed, the wind and whistling stopped, and she collapsed on the floor, shivering and shaking and rubbing her arms and legs for warmth."

"What a horrible ordeal!" Dad commented, finishing his drink.

"Did Josalynn and the pilot make it to safety?"

"Yes, but Doug was gone. He must have been blown out of the utility door and landed into the ocean. His body was never found and was washed up on shore months later."

"I can't believe that his body could survive after falling from a plane," Mom nodded, wondering.

"They claim that he fell through the icy tundra and froze beneath it, which kept his body preserved. Then he thawed out in the spring and washed up on shore," I said, shaking just thinking about it.

"I have read stories where people were covered in snow and survived," Dad commented.

"Doug must have died when he hit the ice and only his body survived," I guessed.

My parents stayed for a few more hours and were impressed by what I had done to the house. They looked around the yard, walked on a few nature trails, and strolled along the beach. The ferryboat arrived and we took it to the mainland where we parted. When I returned to the house, a beautiful woman stood on the terrace and waved. She was dressed in a plaid dress, a thin beige blouse, and a sun hat. Her long hair glistened as a light breeze brushed the strands across her shoulders.

"Katy, how are you?" I called, approaching her.

"I am doing well," she commented, smiling.

"It is such a pleasure to see you," I said, grasping her arm.

"You are also looking good despite what you have gone through in the last couple of days," she said, moving my arm.

"Yes, it has been quite an ordeal dealing with the death of Marcus and Josalynn."

"Yes, that was a horrible tragedy. I heard about the drowning," she sympathized.

"What brings you here?" I wondered.

"I came to visit you a few days ago, but you were not here. I was a bit worried. I talked to Father Leonard and he informed that you were on an island mourning for them. I am so sorry," she said sincerely. "Is there anything I can do?"

"No, just seeing you is enough. It brightens my day," I said.

She turned and dodged my glance. "I came here to let you know that I am going back to New York."

"Katy, I hate to see you go. You are always welcome to stay here."

"I appreciate the offer," she commented, looking out to sea.

"Do you feel a lot better now that you have closure?"

She thought for a moment and nodded, "Yes, I do."

"I still don't understand why you wanted to leave this place. You seem so content here."

"I have my reasons," she commented.

"Don't you miss any of this?"

"There are places like this in New York," she told me.

"But not like this place," I said.

She smiled without a comment.

"Did your husband ever come to visit you in New York?"

She cringed and her body seemed to tighten as she spoke. "He was supposed to come and visit me. He was coming by plane but never showed up," she said sadly.

"Why, what happened?" I inquired.

"I think he fell from the plane. I am not sure," she said fidgeting and sweating.

"Did you ever think of coming back here to visit him?"

"No, I told you I could not handle the loneliness and heartbreak of being away from my family. He lost his parents at an early age and didn't have any brothers or sisters. I grew up with a large family."

"I am surprised they never wanted to come here for a visit or vacation," I said, trying to understand.

She paused a few minutes looking for an answer. "They are allergic to sun and sea water. They break out in hives. My sister is definitely afraid of sea creatures," she said.

"I can understand that. My best friend Colin can't handle the sun and burns fast."

"It makes me feel good to know that this place will have someone living in it who can make a difference and bring more peace and tranquility to the lives of others," she said, looking into my eyes.

"I will try my best," I smiled.

"I don't understand exactly what you do, yet I can sense a beautiful aura around you. I know what you are doing is good and meaningful. This was not a happy place when I lived here."

"I am sure Doug did his best to make it livable," I said, trying to raise her spirits.

Something happened and a horrible rage came over her. "He made this place a living hell!"

Her outburst caught me by surprise.

"Doug was a drunk and a wife beater. I never wanted to leave this place and loved the ocean. I thought that if I came back here, things would change, yet all it did was bring back the past. Joah, it was horrible. I tried so hard to be a good wife. He was never content about anything," she wept.

"Katy, I am so sorry. I did not know any of this," I said, embracing her. I pushed her hair away from her face and looked into her tear-drenched eyes. She cried hysterically. I tried to console her and my emotions took over and I kissed her. She kissed me back and we were glued to each other in a sacred bond. Our special moment ended as she pulled away from me. "No, this cannot happen. It must not happen," she said, covering her mouth with her hand. She ran across the deck, down the stairs, and onto the beach. I chased her for a while and then stopped. I was uncertain and afraid of what this emotion was all about. Something happened between us, and maybe it was something I hoped would happen even though I was still confused about it. I returned to the house and took a cold shower. My mind was preoccupied and I was alarmed when someone knocked on the wooden enclosure of the outside shower. I turned off the water faucets and looked over, "Hello," I said, recognizing the guy as Officer Jenkins.

"Hey, Joah, I hate to disturb you," he apologized, "but it is important."

"No problem," I answered, dressing in a tank top and shorts. "What brings you here?" I wondered, drying my hair.

"Is there somewhere we can talk?"

"Sure, follow me," I said, showing him to a wooden bench near the dock.

"I was so sorry to hear about the death of Marcus and Josalynn," he sympathized, sitting.

"Yes, that was an unfortunate accident," I said, sitting next to him.

"That is not why I am here," he told me, fidgeting.

I waited in anticipation for him to continue.

"Do you know a Marty Fredricks?"

"Yes, I met him at a novelty store," I explained.

"We arrested him today for charge-card theft," Officer Jenkins explained.

"I am sorry to hear about it."

"It was your charge card," he said, showing it to me.

I lowered my head in disappointment and embarrassment. "I can't believe he swiped it from me."

"You have a right to press charges against him," he explained.

"Let me talk to him first. I will go to the police station with you."

"That will be fine," the officer agreed.

I dressed in casual shorts and a pull-over logo T-shirt. We waited for the taxi boat and took it to the mainland. The officer led me to the police station and had me wait in a disgusting waiting room. A stench of sweat and dirt filled the air. Strings of webs hung from the ceilings and fans. There were many strange-looking people scattered around the room. It seemed like an eternity until they called my name. I filled out a few forms, was checked for positive ID, and was issued a card. I was escorted back to the waiting room.

There was strange music playing and re-runs of CSI on the television. I was confused and not certain what to say to him. I got my thoughts together and prepared myself for this confrontation. A door squeaked and a woman showed me to a small room and informed me that I would be watched through a window and that our conversation would be taped. I agreed and was escorted down a long dark corridor by a security guard with a gun. He opened a door and let me into a small room with several chairs and locked it. Marty was sitting in a chair with his head bent in embarrassment. I sat across from him and said, "Hello." At first he didn't answer and I felt like a ghost.

"What do you want?" he snapped.

"That is a nice greeting," I commented.

He lifted his head and flung a dirty look at me. "Most people who come to see me want to see me dead. You got your revenge and your charge card back, so what else do you want?"

"An apology would be nice," I said.

He sat silently, unenthused, uninterested, and unresponsive.

"Marty, why are you so hard on yourself?"

"I have learned to be tough and unfeeling. It is part of living on the street," he said, gritting his teeth.

"I have an ultimatum," I explained.

"And what might that be?" Marty snickered.

"Come and stay with me. You need a fatherly figure to help you straighten out your life and get you on the right track," I told him.

"You are out of your freaking mind!" he muttered.

"It is either that or spend more time in juvenile hall."

"I don't want to spend time in another dysfunctional home," he wept.

"I will try to keep you in a functional family," I promised.

"And don't think I am going to be another victim to the other side," he informed me.

"That will be fine," I promised.

"I am not really sure about all of this," he said with uncertainty.

"I am not pressing charges. I could have had you arrested long ago, so think about that. You are free to go and waste your life away," I said, leaving my chair and going to the door.

"Wait, I will stay with you."

It was the answer I was hoping to hear. It took several days to get the finalized papers together They put him under my custody since he had no family and no where else to go, and they gave me a social worker to inform me about all of his problems. If he got into any more trouble or was arrested, he would be taken away from me and placed in a juvenile prison or detention home. The social worker brought the very few things he owned and placed them into Marsh's old room. My health was getting worse and new pains were developing each day.

There was someone fumbling below with a black suitcase and a beach umbrella. He hid his face from the sun and got everything situated, a chair and blanket, and shuffled through the sand. He placed sunblock on his face and looked up at me.

"Hello, Colin," I waved, walking across the deck and down the stairs to join him.

"How have you been doing?" he asked, rubbing the lotion on his face.

"I am okay," I answered, ducking beneath the umbrella.

"Did you pick up the frames from the novelty shop?"

"Yes, I did," I answered.

"Good. I have some new photos I want to put into them," he said, grasping his black bag.

I was uncertain whether to tell him about the robbery now or later. I followed him up the stairs to the terrace and showed him into the house. There was a long silence as Colin circled around the room.

"I guess you did not like the way I placed all of the photos and pictures. They are all moved. Where are all of the framed photos of the movie stars?" he asked hysterically.

"I was robbed and some of them are missing."

"Oh my God!" he said breathlessly. "Are you all right?"

"Yes, I was not here when I was robbed."

"Did you tell the police?"

"Yes, I was at the station today to file a report."

"Who would do such a thing?"

"I would," a voice echoed from the stairway.

"Who is this?" he stuttered.

"I am Marty. I stole some of your movie-star memorabilia and sold it so I could have money for drugs," he answered, walking down the stairs.

"And you are letting him stay here? Are you nuts?"

"I also stole his charge card and bought more drugs, and you know what this man did? He forgave me and is letting me stay with him. It is going to take time for me to get my life together, but with the help of Joah, I think I can do it."

Colin glared at Marty, speechless, and circled the room. "I have to change some of these photos. They don't look right."

"Thanks for understanding," I told Colin, grasping his shoulder.

"It is always something new with you," he smiled.

"Colin, I am really sorry," Marty apologized. "I made a mess of things. Don't blame Joah. I tore this place apart and took what I could for cash. I will make it up to both of you someday. It was very wrong of me and I feel really bad. I have hurt both of you," he explained.

"Don't be so hard on yourself," I told Marty.

"You can help me straighten this all out," Colin said, handing Marty a hammer and nails.

"I would love to help. Thanks," he said.

Colin directed him on what to do and how to hang the framed photos.

I fixed us each a glass of lemonade to drink and dragged Colin away from Marty and onto the beach.

"Where are we going? Should we leave him alone in the house?"

"He will be fine," I reassured Colin.

"I would be a nervous wreck if I had someone like him in my house."

"I think he has ambition and will change," I told Colin.

"Why did he have to take my prized photos?" Colin said, kicking piles of sand on the beach, almost spilling his drink.

"Can we just forget about the incident for a while?" I pleaded.

"I guess so," Colin said, clutching his umbrella.

We found a private beach and set up a blanket and umbrella. The waves pounded on the shore and cast a refreshing mist around us. "Katy came to see me the other day."

"Is she going to stay on the island?"

"No, she is leaving for New York," I explained, sipping.

"For some reason I thought she would stay on the island. She seems to really like it here."

"I was really surprised to see her," I told him, grinning.

"Well, she is a beautiful woman," Colin answered, licking his lips.

"It was very thoughtful of her to give me this house. I thought for sure she would move in with me or stay for a while."

"I did too," he said, finishing his lemonade.

"I thought it was loneliness, the death of her husband, or the destruction of the house after the hurricane that pushed her away, but it was something completely different."

Colin looked at me with confusion, stunned. "Then what was it?"

"I will tell you someday," I thought, not wanting to blurt out what really happened to her. I was not sure if she would want anyone else to know what her husband had done to her.

"Did something happen between the two of you?" Colin guessed.

I thought about his question and shook my head."No, but someday I hope it does."

Colin smacked my shoulder and said. "I hope so too. Thanks again for turning me on to the ocean," he grinned.

The whistle of the ferryboat sounded in the distance. Everyone I knew had been part of a voyage or trip—Marsh, Mum, Marcus, Josalynn. Their time was done, but Colin, Marty, and I were just beginning a new journey along with Katy, Father Leonard, and my family, and there was no turning back. I would never turn back and was ready for the trials and tribulations ahead of me.

Printed in the United States
200266BV00001B/175-363/A